THE MAGENDRA

VOLUME ONE

BY DANA WITHAM

DORRANCE
PUBLISHING CO
EST. 1920
PITTSBURGH, PENNSYLVANIA 15238

Dorrance Publishing Co
585 Alpha Drive
Suite 103
Pittsburgh, PA 15238
Visit our website at *www.dorrancebookstore.com*

ISBN: 979-8-8860-4175-0
eISBN: 979-8-8860-4831-5

THE MAGENDRA

VOLUME ONE

To my lovely wife Kristen.

You are the spark of this world;
without your love of stories, this
would not exist.

Chapter One

Awake to Nothing

The hot afternoon crushed down on my throbbing head as I opened my eyes to the scorching sun. The flies had started to collect around me. The shadow of a buzzard blocked the sun's rays for a half-second before the burning heat returned to my face. Struggling and sore, I begin the long journey to vertical, staggering only a little after a long minute.

Oh God, what happened? As the fog clears from my head a little, I realize that I have no recollection of where I am or how I got here. *Did I fall?* As I look at my surroundings, I realize I am on a sandy, flat-topped hill with steep slopes on three sides and a gradual slope down in front of me. The area is about 400 feet across with 30-foot canyon walls of reddish-brown stone. The hill is nestled in the center of the canyon, the walls rising on three sides. *A box canyon? What the hell, where am I?* As I search myself for some clue of what is going on, I find nothing, nothing at all, then the hard rush of adrenaline that surges through my body adds to the creeping panic, *who am I?!*

With no recollection of anything, I turn my attention to the details of myself, grasping for any possible clue. My clothes are dirty and a little torn in some places. Coarse sand and brush burns cover me, adding to my confusion. My tan leather hiking boots seem a little too tight due to the heat and my swollen feet. My blue, plaid, sleeveless shirt is dirty and torn in several places, with what looks like bloodstains, possibly from the brush burns that cover the better part of my visible skin. My khaki shorts pockets, empty, aside from the sand filling the bottoms, hold no clues to who I am. Searching around for a possible bag or purse reveals nothing, only the long drag path leading to where I stand.

At further inspection, I noticed footprints in the dry, sandy dirt, leading down the sloped path along with the drag marks. Touching my tender elbows, I realize the drag path was made by my previously unconscious body.

The thought of it instantly infuriates me, and the hot sun and sore body weren't helping my attitude any. Letting out a long, angry breath, I begin following the only way out of this treacherous canyon. Examining the large boot prints that entered and exited the canyon beside where my body was dragged, I can't help but think of what I would do to my assailant if I was lucky enough to run into that bastard!

After walking slowly and laboriously down the path for about ten minutes, the decline of the slope starts to increase dramatically, causing every step to become a painful jar every time my boots hit the ground. The buzzing from the cicadas and waves of nausea starts adding to my annoyance. My mouth is as dry as the desert, and I can't spit. My world lurches as the dizziness hits, my body rejecting the simple action of walking. I stumble over my own feet, tripping myself into a face-first tumble down the path.

Ow! Son of a… My knees bounce off of stones. *Dirty!* … More stones, more dirt. My tumble finally ends, leaving me even more sore than I thought possible. *Am I at the bottom of the path now?!* As I look up, the canyon walls seem to be breaking into large stones and sparse juniper trees. The dizziness starts to subside as I lay there, unfortunately, the newly found pain does not! There are trees though, promising shade from the burning sun. *All I have to do is get back up!* After a small, quiet tantrum, I gather myself back up again.

Finding tire tracks leading across the flatter country, my anger begins to slowly fade into logic. *I'm sure I'll find a road connected to those tracks.* I pick up a sturdy stick from a nearby juniper, hoping to keep myself off the ground.

The growing need for water starts to spur my advance cross-country, the low hills molding into an expanse of trees and short grass. The shade feels good and I think I can see a road in spots through the overgrowth of sage. *Finally, now we are getting somewhere!* I feel a surge of relief to find that the road looks well-traveled, only a dirt road, but it holds more comfort than the goat path out of the canyon. *Now, what way do I go? Come on pick it, left or right. Okay, okay, right then.*

As small plumes of dust rise from under my boots, I am on the road traveling to the right, it feels like north to me somehow. It isn't going with the sun, which seems to be on a downward arc. *I'm pretty sure it's afternoon but not by much*, I think.

As I travel, my mind starts to wander. I imagine a car or truck cruising down the road. I try to imagine anything about myself: my home, my past, anything to take my mind off my dry, parched mouth and achy body. Then, my mind turns to darker thoughts of being dragged off into a desert canyon by some big, faceless man who left those large prints that I had seen. "God, who did I piss off?" I said aloud, maybe to break that annoying buzzing coming from the brushy overgrowth along the road. *Well, my voice and imagination still work*, I think, *at least that's something!*

The road starts a gradual curve to the left and downhill slightly. The trees seem to be getting larger and the shrubbery denser. Taller grasses replace the stunted brown clumps that previously littered the landscape. I must have managed five miles by now, and the walking is becoming easier on the downward slope. *Hopefully, the lack of water won't catch up with me before I can find some help.*

Before I manage a prayer, the road straightens, and my attention is captured by five small brown spots moving around slowly in the road, about 200 yards ahead of me. *What are they, rats?* As I get closer, the small brown spots turn out to be some type of short-haired pigs that are squeaking and rummaging near the edge of the road, now only about thirty feet away. They don't seem scared, probably consumed by the search for whatever is at the road edge. Only fifteen feet away now. *They seem fearless, what are they?* About eight feet away, I make a run for it. My boots pound on the ground as I run past the now squealing creatures.

I make it only two feet past them when a loud, lower squeal comes from the bushes, with the sound of snapping sagebrush. A larger, hairy pig bursts out into the road, heading right toward me. I ready my makeshift walking stick, swing it like a ball bat, trying to intercept the charging pig, which is as big as a medium-sized dog, and I hit nothing but air.

"Ahhh, bastard!" I scream as the small tusks dig deep into my calf. Panic-stricken, I swing again, taking the creature firm in the side with a low thud and a loud snap as my walking stick broke under the force of the blow. The animal squeals off in the direction of the babies.

With the damage done, I limp down the road away from the lessening noise of the angry, mother pig, trailing a little blood until I find a place to sit and mend my bleeding leg. I tear a bit of my shirt off to clean and bind the wound. *That should do until I can get some kind of antiseptic. What are the chances? When will my luck change?*

I sigh before finally getting back onto my feet. Leaving my broken walking stick where it lays, I continue on my previous path. I hear what sounds like water in the distance. I start to eagerly quicken my pace, ignoring the sharp pain in my leg every step, thinking only of my parched mouth and near-bleeding lips. Before I can make it to the water, an engine roaring up behind me spurs a new surge of adrenaline. Out of terror that it might be my assailant, I dart to the nearest bush off the side of the road to hide, knowing I could never take him on in the shape I'm in now, or even outrun him, for that matter.

I crouch as low as I possibly can, keeping my balance and a good enough stance, in case I have to make a run for it. A gray Chevy Stepside finally makes its way around the bend to where I can see that a young man is driving with a young woman at his side. Two other women and one man are riding in the bed of the truck. Their music is blaring "...sweet home Alabama, Lord, I'm coming home to you..." along with yells of excitement from the riders in the back.

They passed quickly, kicking up dust, and then they were out of sight. I can still hear them pretty clearly, as they stopped in the direction of the water. I get out of my uncomfortable crouch, moving slowly toward the small party, and, hopefully, the water that I need so badly. Finally, I make it to where I can see one man and one woman lying on a picnic blanket, with a small cooler in front of the truck. The other three already swimming in the wide, green-colored creek.

Approaching the group shyly, clearing my throat to get their attention. The man on the blanket, with medium blond hair and a complexion lighter than I expected for this heat and sun, looks up. "Hi," he says with a grimaced look, "Are you okay?" The thin, blond lady sitting beside him gasps when she sees my appearance. Quickly brushing off some excess dirt and sand, I reply, "Uhh... yeah, I'm okay. Just been having a rough day. Umm... do you have some water I could have, please?" The fellow says, "Sure."

The woman quickly got up and grabbed a bottle out of the cooler, handing it to me, looking me up and down again. I gratefully took the bottle, attempting to drink slowly, as I down almost half of it, feeling a bit of nausea immediately. As the crowd in the water silenced, the man on the blanket stood up, introducing himself. "My name is Carl, this is my fiancée, Gina."

After a slight pause, I replied, "I'm Susan," thinking to myself, *at least I know these people won't be able to tell that I made that up on the fly.* "Do you need a ride somewhere? You're welcome to stay here with us to catch a ride back to town if you'd like to," says Carl.

Gina quickly chimes in, "What happened to you, dear? You don't look so good. How did you get all of those brush burns? And that bloody bandage... what did you use?" Looking up, she saw my torn shirt, realizing what I had used. "What happened to you?" she asked again, with a look of concern.

I stammered as I started thinking about what would be believable, yet keep me out of danger's way. "A... four-wheeler accident... I rolled it... and blew a tire... and I think one of the front springs might be busted." Carl asks nicely, "Would you like to go pick it up on our way back into town?" "I think she probably wants to pick it up later. She needs to see a doctor first, with all that blood coming from her leg," says Gina.

As a rush of relief came sailing through me, *thank you, Gina, thank you!* Carl replies to his fiancée, "Yeah, you're probably right, hon." After looking down at my leg, he nodded to his friend in the water. "James, let's get moving, we'll come back later." Gina nods in agreement, seeming thankful to be rid of me.

James and the other two ladies climb out of the water, making their way to the towels hung up on a nearby tree. They all walked over, towels wrapped around their dripping bodies, to introduce themselves as Carl started packing up. James sticks out his hand, "My name is James, haven't seen you around before."

The two ladies walk up, giggling between themselves, obviously younger than the rest of the group, and I realize that they are twins, surprisingly. As they got a closer look at me, their giggling ceases, replaced by a bit of concerned shock due to my current sorry condition. "Hello, I'm Jane." "And I'm Julia." Carl just finished packing the truck and said, "I think we're good," motioning to the rest to get in the back, and, momentarily, we're heading back into town, in the direction in which I came.

Good thing I ran into these guys, who knows how long I would've been walking. Ahh, this is so much better than walking! I began to relax as soon as the truck got up to speed. I finished my bottle of water, then I leaned up against the side of the truck bed, feeling the wind rushing through my hair, blowing off the loose dirt, and drying my sweat. Then, I realized the twins were staring at me relentlessly, not having anything to say. *Oh God, here we go!* James also noticed Jane and Julia staring. He asked, "So Susan, where do you live?"

Thinking I was in the clear with these guys, I had to scramble again for another answer. "I'm here on vacation, I'm from Ohio." "How long are you staying for?" asks James. Abruptly, the back window slides open, with Gina saying loudly, "How are you doing back there, dearie? Would you like another water?" I gratefully accept the outstretched water, as Gina continues, "We're gonna drop you off right at the hospital if that's okay with you." She is not making it a question at all. I nod in agreement and slump back against the side of the truck with an exhausted grunt, hoping to deflect any more questions from any of the passengers.

We ride the rest of the way in silence, with nothing but the wind and tires on pavement as we turn onto the highway, going a swift sixty-five miles per hour.. I used this time, trying to regain any memory, checking every road sign for recollection and clues of my whereabouts. *Oh, dizzy!* **Rt 95.** *Nausea.* **Boulder City Nevada.** *What the hell?!*

Everything was starting to look like a black and white movie, *I must hang on a little longer!* Boulder City fifteen miles? *Oh my god, I have no idea what's going on!* "HEY, GUYS! I think she's passing out..." Darkness consumed me, except for moments that seemed to wave in and out. Time was no longer relevant, only movement was.

There was a hard bump. *What the...?* As the lights flash past me, I see someone standing over me, "You're going to be okay, just hang on." "I need an IV here and a CT stat!" I felt the needle go in. *Ouch! God, I'm so tired!* Darkness! Buzz, buzz, feeling the CT scanner for a moment as I drift in and out of consciousness.

CHAPTER TWO

A Twist of Fate and a Near Escape

Drip… Drip… Drip. *Oh man, what's going on now?* Opening my eyes just a crack, I catch the setting sun through the half-open blinds. The hospital bed felt amazing on my aching body, the first bit of comfort I could remember. Drip… drip, *but what's that sound? And for that matter, where is that hissing coming from?*

The loud talking from the doorway started to get annoying. Turning toward the door to tell whoever it was that my head still hurt, and could they keep it down… *the door's shut?*

Drip… Drip. Looking over to the sound and found it easily, a saline drip! *How the hell can I hear that?*

I felt weird. Every time I looked at an area of the room, I could almost feel my body move in the direction that I was looking. Must be the drugs I was given for pain, but for some reason, I couldn't convince myself of that. I felt better, but the pain was still present.

Ok, let's see… moving my leg to the edge of the bed, *yep, things seem to be working. And the other leg now!* Without too much trouble, I was sitting on the side of the bed. Hissss, the baseboard heat was starting to sound like a teapot as the water flowed through more rapidly as the thermostat kicked on with a loud click. The talk outside seemed to become louder, as I looked up at the door. It sounded like the state police.

"We have no one of that description on the missing-persons list, did you get the license plate number of the people who dropped her off?" I moved a little to the left to see the secretary sitting at the desk through the window in the door... *On the phone?! No way I'm hearing this!*

"No sir, like I said, they told me, she was walking out in the desert, upstream from Lake Mohave when they found her. She was injured, so they brought her in. They said she passed out about ten minutes prior to arrival. They also said her name is Susan, and she's from Ohio. That's all we got. No ID, no personal effects."

"Okay, I'll send an officer up tomorrow to try to make a positive ID, and we will go from there," said the voice of the police officer. "Thank you, officer. You have a good night." Click. The phone hung up. *Wow, holy crap!* The shock of what I had just experienced hit me. Before I could collect myself a new burst of intuition. *And now, the doctor!* Almost like clockwork, the secretary looks up...

"Hello Doctor Noland, how are you?" "Fine Colleen. How's our patient in 313 doing?" says Dr. Noland. "She was sleeping well about thirty minutes ago." "Well, I'm making my final rounds for the night then going to get some rest. It has been a more than interesting day!"

Quickly, I tipped my head down as the doctor's attention turned to the door. "Oh good, it looks like she's awake, I'll be a few minutes Colleen." *And here we go again!*

The doctor knocks and comes in. "Good evening young lady." Doctor Noland looked to be in his late sixties, with balding white hair that appeared to have long lost its last hints of any color. He wore a pair of thin, rectangular, wire-framed reading glasses that set low on his nose, making it easy for him to peer over the top of them, which he did often. Complimenting his nose was a large, fuzzy, white mustache, larger than expected for a man in his profession.

"How are you feeling?" Dr. Noland asked. "I feel much better now." "That's good to hear; you have been out for a while. I have a few questions that I need you to answer for me about your situation. It seems that the folks helping you couldn't give us adequate information to make a proper medical file on you, so if we could start with your name?"

What to do!? "Well doctor, I can't tell you any information, because to tell you the truth, I can't remember anything but waking up out in the God-forsaken desert with nothing at all!" *Well, there you go, come right out with the truth. I don't know how smart that was! Too late now!* "The people that dropped you off told us that your name is Susan and that you are here on vacation from Ohio."

"I wish that were the case doctor, but I felt like I had to come up with something. I get this feeling like something really bad happened to me to get me into this situation, and I really am not embracing the virtue of trust right now!" Doctor Noland looked intently at his clipboard for a moment. "I can respect that notion, ma'am. Maybe if you get a bit more rest, it will come back to you. In the meantime, we will do the best we can to ensure your health and safety. If it's okay with you, I will schedule a few more tests tomorrow and see what we can do about getting you to the appropriate people to help you."

"Am I okay, doctor?" "Well, your vitals and lab work came back normal, but your CT scan came back inconclusive, so we did further testing. There were some abnormalities on your EEG. I believe that is due to a moderate concussion." *He's lying, he's trying to hide something.*

"We will run more testing tomorrow to confirm. So, if you're feeling better, I'll have the nurse remove the IV." "Yes doctor, thank you." "Alright, get some rest, and I'll see you tomorrow."

As the doctor walked to the door, I felt as if something was amiss. I had the sensation of impending doom throughout my entire body. I try to let my mind wander, but the only place of thought that it had to wander to was my current situation. I heard the doctor tell the nurse that I would no longer need the IV and that it could be removed, but it didn't make me feel any better since they were at the other end of the hall and my door was closed!

What is happening to me? Although my real question was: what was *going* to happen to me? Within minutes, the nurse arrived at my door and knocked.

"Hi my name is Rachele, I'll be your nurse for the night. I came to remove your IV." I nodded my head and put my arm out. Rachele was a short, chubby nurse with glasses and frizzy, short, dark brown hair who seemed to smile a lot even if there was nothing to smile about. "There you go dear; if there is anything you need just ring the bell!" I said thank you, and she headed for the door leaving me alone with my thoughts.

'Get some rest' she says. Hah, no chance in that right now! It sounded like most of the people had left for the night. Looking at the clock, I see that it is 9:55 P.M. I got out of bed and strode across the room to the cabinets, opened the door, and found my clothes and boots sitting neatly on the shelf.

I took out my shirt, which was in poor shape. I carefully removed the rest of the torn bottom that I had used for my tourniquet, turning it into a makeshift belly shirt, which was much better. I took the rest of my clothes into the bathroom and cleaned them up as much as I could, removing nearly half a cup of sand! *Why is this happening to me?*

After replacing my clothes in the cabinet, I lay down and finally felt sleep start to creep in on me. A man sat behind a large desk, silhouetted by dim firelight. His head was tilted down with his arms on the desk. Looking at some papers, his curly dark hair hung down a little, shading his features. He was wearing a dark blue collared shirt with two buttons unfastened, showing the shine of gold in the flickering light, possibly a necklace.

"We have a patient coming up from the ER…" "Good morning." "…just took the IV out." *What the…?* I snapped awake abruptly to the sounds of people talking and a variety of noise clutter. 6:45 A.M. God, that was fast. The morning had snuck up on me. Within seconds, the worry was back. *What am I gonna do?!* It sounds like the shifts are changing.

"Lori, our patient in 313 is scheduled for an EEG at 7:30. Be sure to page me when she goes down to the lab, I want to be there for this." "Okay, Doctor Noland." "Oh yeah, Doctor Lamonté from psychiatry should be here around that time as well. Will you let him know I'm downstairs?" "Yes, I will Doctor." "Thank you, Lori."

Oh, I gotta get out of here! My stomach churned. *I need some kind of plan, but I have nothing!*

Click! The door opens and in walks an elderly nurse, "good morning, dear. My name is Hazel, I'll be your nurse for the day. How are you feeling?" "I'm a little overwhelmed, to tell you the truth." My eyes turned to fire as a hot tear rolled down my cheek. The nurse's eyes sparkled with true sympathy as she looks down, seeming to look for the right words to ease my anguish. I got the feeling that she really wanted to help me.

Hazel looked up forcing a smile and composing herself. "Oh, my poor dear, you have been put through the wringer, haven't you? Not to worry honey, you'll just be getting a repeat test, and I'm sure you'll be fine." It was the nicest lie I was ever told, the little voice in my head told me. *Damn it must be bad!*

"I'll take you down, and I'll be right there when you're done. The wheelchair is right out here in the hallway." As I started to get up, the phone rang. "Hello, this is Lori." I hear the voice of Doctor Noland on the other end, as my keen hearing kicked back in, though I hadn't realized that it had ever quit.

"Can you tell Hazel to entertain our patient in 313 for a while, the EEG machine seems to have malfunctioned, and it could take hours for the tech to get here."

Excitement jumped in my chest! "I sure can, Doctor." "Thank you, Lori." "Hazel, please report to the nurse's station," the intercom rattled. Already on my feet, Hazel shot me a quick smile and said, "That's me, honey, make yourself comfortable, and I'll be back shortly."

She turned and walked out, closing the door behind her. *Get comfortable she says!* So, I briskly trotted to the cabinet, got my clothes, and zipped to the bathroom. Moments, later I was dressed and looking no worse for the wear. *God, what I would give for a handbag!*

Waiting for what seemed to be an eternity, I could hear Hazel and the secretary chatting.

"But I don't know what to do in this situation, she is having a rough time Lori, and I don't know what to tell her!" "Just think of something Hazel, your guess is as good as mine!" "Well, here goes nothing." I put on my best expression of ignorance, hoping that my excitement wouldn't show. *Okay distress, not excitement. My stomach lurched again, there that helps! Now for those tears!*

It wasn't too difficult; as Hazel knocked on the door and entered, the tears welled up in my eyes. "It seems it may be a while before you can get your test, the machine seems to have malfunctioned." The tears rolled down my cheeks

"God, how much more of this do I have to take, I'm just so stressed out with this whole situation!" Daring to take a quick glance at the clock, I see that it is 8:00 A.M. "I just don't know what to do, when will it be fixed?" "The doctor says it could take several hours dear." "And what am I supposed to do for several hours?"

Hazel looked at the floor for a few moments pondering my proposal, then she looked up at me with a smile. "Why don't you go down to the cafeteria and have an ice cream, dear? That always makes me feel better when I'm having a time of it. Yes, that's what you should do! Just take the elevator to the first floor and go to the left, you can't miss the sign."

I sobbed and looked up with the slightest smile. "Really? It does sound good." "I'll walk you to the elevator, my dear." Letting out I sigh of relief, Hazel and I headed out the door into the hall. The hall was nearly empty and the secretary Lori smiled at Hazel as she patted me on the shoulder and led me down the hall. Turning the corner, I saw the elevators at the end of the hall. My adrenaline had a mind of its own as it started to pump harder with every step.

Just stay calm, just a little farther! Hazel had been telling me something, but I didn't pick up on the conversation until she said she would see me in a few minutes. I pushed the button and then DING! "Thank you, Hazel." "You are very welcome, dear. Enjoy your ice cream." Seconds later, I was headed down the hall, looking for an exit that wasn't too busy. *Ophthalmology, yep, an empty waiting room and an exit, just keep walking.*

As the door swung open, a gust of hot dry air hit me, and I breathed in the free air again. I quickly moved across the small landscaped courtyard to the sidewalk and headed out toward nowhere, and I couldn't bring myself to care where I was going! *Boulder City, huh? Doesn't seem like much! Well, I suppose that's a good thing.*

It seems like it's only been an hour since I got out of that hospital, and it's already twenty degrees hotter than it was then. The heat was starting to bite in again. *Oh, my world for a Pepsi,* which at this point didn't amount to much. Thoughts of money floated in my mind, just out of my grasp, it seemed. The dry gravel on the side of the road crunched under my feet; it was loud, and the rhythmic sound was starting to get annoying. My thirst started to add to the annoyance, and then…

Whoa! What the…? A sudden sensation stopped me; it was almost a chill. The drainage grate caught my attention, then my eyes adjusted, and I noticed the small green corner of paper protruding from the edge of the grate. *No! I don't believe it!* Covering the fifteen feet in three strides, I bent down and gently tugged the small green corner of the paper, and gasped as the folded up ten-dollar bill came loose. Standing up quickly, looking around, clutching the money to my chest, I surveyed my surroundings and… Nobody! Feeling my face stretch into a big grin helped me feel invigorated again after the adrenaline dumping hours prior. *Pepsi!*

Chapter Three

Lucky

What happened to me? I wish I had some clue as to the mystery of myself. *Why were they treating me so strangely? What was wrong with my EEG? Well, everything has been strange since I walked out of that canyon. God! I'm the most unlucky and lucky individual that can exist! It can't be imagination, something is going on, but I don't even know who I am. I should be turning myself into the funny farm!*

The sense of myself and my mental status seemed so sharp as I walked toward my next destination, almost like I knew where I was going. A feeling of confidence easily battered its way through the confusion. *Ha! I'm making myself feel confused because I know that's what I should be feeling. And what is this crazy self-analysis?*

God, how can I feel like I should just go with it, how can I convince myself this is all a good thing? Somewhere in my subconscious, it felt like everything was okay with me, that things were the way they should be. Even though I was really confused, I had a strange sense of comfort. *There it is, the Exxon sign… Why is that the place to be?* I had a strong feeling that I needed to be there.

Ding! The electric chime on the door rang as I walked into the gas station's mini-mart. An obese guy, looking to be in his twenties, sat behind the counter eating Cheetos. He nodded as I came in and continued munching, as Offspring played on the radio. "Chances thrown, nothings free, longing for what used to be." *Perfect sense,* I thought, as the guy's past flashed through my mind. *NO! I shouldn't know that!* But I did.

Walking to the back, I snatched a Pepsi from the cooler, staring directly at the row of slot machines up against the wall farther in the back, feeling them stare back. *It can't be, I don't believe myself!*

As I headed to the counter, the big guy let out a breath of agitation as he got up and said, "A dollar five, please," giving me my change with his fat Cheeto-stained fingers. *They will just hire anyone here,* I thought. But somehow, I knew he was the owner's son and the regular attendant was taking some time off for his expecting wife. *I am a nut job!*

Going to leave, at the door, I turned abruptly about two feet away and walked directly back to the One-Armed Bandit machine in the back, the third one from the end... clink, clink! The quarter rattled into the machine, *now pull!* Whirr, as the reels spun clicking into position. The machine's lights flashed as five-dollar tokens rattled out.

I opened my Pepsi then dropped a dollar token into the machine as I sat down on the cushion-covered stool. Still hearing the crunching of Cheetos behind the desk, I thought, *that's bag number three for him, I bet.* The lights flashed again as another twenty dollar token came rattling out of the machine *And, here we go! This is gonna be a good one!*

Clink, clink, whirr, I watched intently as the symbols clicked into place, one, two, three. Weeehooo!! Weeehooo!! The siren on the machine screamed. My stool hit the floor with a bang. The adrenaline pumped through me. Lights flashed against the walls and ceiling. The rattle of the wheeled chair and the sudden absence of the crunching of Cheetos behind the counter proved that I wasn't the only one startled. *The Jackpot, it's the Jackpot!*

Looking at the sign that said "See attendant for the jackpot," I grabbed my twenty-four-dollar tokens and went to the counter, still shaking from the sudden surprise. And I knew what was about to happen. The big guy was standing behind the counter with a look of total surprise and disgust at the same time. "I've never seen anyone win more than ten dollars on those," he said. "Well, I guess they gotta pay someday, don't they?" I responded.

He just shook his head back and forth a couple of times as he headed to the office to the left of the counter, muttering about people making issues for him and it not being his day, thinking it was low enough that I wouldn't hear.

He came back out with a blue bank pouch and opened the drawer, giving me twenty-four dollars and setting the dollar tokens to the side. Then, he picked up the bank pouch and produced $5,000 neatly wrapped in a currency strap. Again, my heart pounded. I felt a little breathless as he handed me the stack of bills.

"Thank you!" I said, trying not to seem too excited, but it sounded a little squeaky, as my voice broke from the excitement! "You're welcome," he said begrudgingly. This time when I headed to the door, I didn't stop, and I didn't dare even look back again! *Augh! I left my Pepsi! Dang! Not going back now! Oh, hell no!*

Deciding to make as much distance as I could, I headed out again, staying as far off the road as the terrain would allow, thinking to myself that I would need to find somewhere to stay since my nice hospital bed was a thing of the past. *And good riddance! That was as close to being admitted and examined as I wanna get!*

Happy to be free still, I continued walking as the sun moved lower into the western sky, and I picked up my pace as I started feeling the air cooling from being out of the direct sun. I braved a venture to the road to read a sign: **Henderson 5 mi**. Somehow, I already knew that.

The street lights were fully lit by the time I made it into town. Taking the alley behind Macy's to keep from attracting attention, my senses told me that there was something more going on.

Looking around, I searched for the disturbance that I was feeling, and there it was. The employee exit door was ajar, standing out as if it were surrounded by neon lights. *And I am up for some late-night shopping! Do I like shopping?* I almost laughed at the absurdity of the question!

Taking a quick look around, I slipped in the back door, leaving it ajar. *Gear! I need gear!* Collecting the items I needed could have become a problem as I walked through the deserted store. Looking at the racks of clothing, *oooh nooo! Don't get distracted by that!* Shaking my head at the idea of browsing, feeling it like second nature. *What I really need is..*A hoodie, boots, backpack, a few shirts and jeans, and other necessities. Stuffing the contents into my backpack, I grabbed a handbag and headed for the door.

God, I can't take it, my conscience won't let me! Turning back around I sped for the front of the store and put five hundred dollars on the counter before heading back to my escape route. Slipping back out the door, the alley was the way I had left it, empty. Closing the door securely, I returned to my original mission- getting some rest.

Not too much later, I was relaxing by a tree in a nearby park, I had decided that the park benches were a bad idea. I didn't need to be questioned by the authorities for being a vagrant; however, at this point, that would be closer to the truth than anything else that I could come up with. Thought of current events swirled around in my head as I started to doze off. Since there didn't seem to be anything else in there for my mind to think about, this caused me a very uneasy feeling as I started to drift from consciousness.

Looking down at the red granite tiles under my feet I took a few steps, the soles of my shoes making small tapping sounds on the clean polished surface. *I'm dreaming.* That part was obvious to me even in my state. *Is this a memory?* Advancing further, it was a house, warm and full of woodwork, the hallway trim was dark hardwood of some type embossed with leaves and vines, the walls were the color of red velvet cake. At the end of the hall, a beautifully carved door. Something familiar about this place as I recalled my dream from my short hospital stay. *I wonder.*

It's time to get moving! The voice in my head was low and quiet, but it was loud enough that I awoke with a jerk. The sun was up, and a jogger was running on the sidewalk. His everyday ritual. *How do I know this stuff!* Collecting myself and putting my hoodie back into my backpack, I started walking again. The heat was picking up quickly. *It's gonna be hot today, I think!*

It was hot, and it didn't take long to get that way as I headed across town. The sidewalk was starting to put off heat mirages, and I could feel the heat going through my boots. My stomach growled menacingly, *well food would be nice!* The town had become much more active in the last hour or so, vehicles and people were out and moving about. *I wouldn't have thought this town had people two hours ago,* I thought as a green Jimmy low rider cruised by with the top off, the bass speakers bumping as it turned the corner. Three guys talking and laughing with ballcaps turned backward occupied the vehicle, one stood up in the back and yelled something in Spanish as the Jimmy hooked a right down the side street. The smell of coffee hit me from somewhere ahead, and then the smell of fries, chili, steak, biscuits, burger, onions, pickles, and lettuce! *Lettuce! I'm smelling lettuce! How am I smelling lettuce!!*

After walking for a few minutes, the source of the smell came into view. It was a corner diner, and from the look of the parking lot, it was moderately busy. At the same time, I started to get an uneasy feeling as I approached the corner, a group of people outside of a house across the street were staring in my direction. They were all dressed in the same jersey and hats, they looked like they were having much too much fun for this time of the day as a strong chemical smell emanated from the open door of the house. *Nine, ten,* I counted, *five on the porch and five in the house,* as I passed by, I didn't give them a glance. *Damn! Three of them got up, they are certainly coming my way,* knowing without even having to look! *Straight to the diner, I don't like this at all!* Keeping my pace as to keep them from catching up, I headed for the diner door, hoping that the number of people at the diner would deter them.

Outside the diner, there was a large clock on a brown painted concrete stand reading 11:26 as I entered. *Good AC in here.* I thought as I made my way to an empty booth by the window, where I had a good view of the street. The eleven people in here talked over their food, as the television over the counter ran commentaries on the sports of the week. The waitress finished writing down an order and headed my way! "Good morning my name is Jean, can I get you a drink?"

"Coffee, please." God, I like coffee, even on a hot day! *Well, I know that much about myself!* As I chuckled inside. The waitress produced a menu setting it in front of me. "I'll be right back to get your order." Shooting me a smile, she headed to the back. As I had guessed, the hats that followed me had parked themselves across the street from the diner. *Damn! Their stalking! What now?* The waitress was on her way back with my coffee already. "Here you go dear, do you need some more time?"

"No, I'll have the special, a chili burger and fries." She wrote the ticket out, then looked up. "Anything else, dear"? "No that's it." "Your order will be up shortly," she said as she headed to the back again. *And I didn't even open the menu, ugh!* Keeping an eye on the thugs across the street, I thought, *well here we go,* as the news special bulletin came up. "Jane doe leaves the hospital, please keep an eye out for a female in her twenties, 5'9" with light brown hair…." *Well, at least they don't have a picture. God! Why are they after me so, just let it go people!*

Just stay calm, act normal. Sipping my coffee, taking some deep breaths trying to keep my calm. I looked around to see if anyone was looking my way.

The old guy at the counter certainly caught the bulletin, but wasn't looking my way at least, and continued watching the sports column.

My food was on its way, and she sat the food in front of me! "Enjoy, dear." "Would it be too much trouble to get the bill now, ma'am?" I got a funny look from the waitress as she produced the bill. "Not at all dear, here you go." After eating about half of my food, I thought, *okay time to pay. Going to the register*! Another waitress tending the back came up and took the bill.

"That will be $9.18, please." After paying with a twenty, I headed back to my table. Folding the tip and putting it neatly under the creamer bowl, I thought *just time for a few more bites*. About three minutes later, the cop car pulled into the diner parking lot. *Yep, the thugs are making a hasty retreat, but not fast enough*. They caught the officer's attention, the squad car peeled out of the parking lot toward them. *They're gonna run!*

An older couple just getting done paying were headed for the door as I fell in behind them, the older fellow holding the door for both his wife and me. "Thank you, sir!" Filing out the further front exit was a great idea, as it made it easy to make it to the side street away from all the action that I didn't need. Turning left, *yeah, this feels like a good way to go*, and counting it as luck again since there wasn't much going on down this way. It was actually pretty quiet down here as I hooked a right. *I need out of this town. I feel like I've worn out my welcome.* Since I came to this town welcome wasn't part of the experience. *Time to move on, like days ago!* chuckling to myself, as the houses started to thin out a bit.

CHAPTER FOUR

Missy

On the outskirts of town, the housing became sparse quickly, and a lot of the residences had been abandoned years ago, by the looks of it. *Looks like these people wore out their welcome long ago as well. Humm, do I like camping? Looks like I'm gonna find out. No way I can go back to town!*

Feeling the truth in my thoughts, I ventured farther away from the town and back out into the high desert, looking for less pavement and attention. I found it in no time, a not heavily traveled but well-maintained dirt road heading farther out of town and still easy walking. The sun was on its way down, and the heat seemed to be easing up a bit. *Walking, nothing but juniper, quiet, suns getting lower. Wish I had that Pepsi! Can't think about this crap anymore!* As I walked for a while I realized I hadn't been thinking about anything! I hadn't had a thought cross my mind for the last hour as I headed to some unknown destination.

Starting to feel a strange sensation at the back of my neck, a steeple and a cross came into view, silhouetted by the setting sun as I made the top of a small incline. *Holy!!! What the!* I got off the road and moved with as much stealth as I could muster, looking around. *Two houses, a church, and a graveyard, and not a soul! Sneaking for a closer look!*

Oh god! Here I go again, should be running in the other direction!! Windows are knocked out, paint is almost gone, well it used to be white! Building up enough courage, I crept over to the church. Slowly taking a peek through one of the broken side windows and…. *Nothing. Nothing but dust and some beer cans.* Checking the rest of the houses with more of the same results, some graffiti, more remanences of parties long past. The graveyard looked like it had been neglected for years, and the caretaker's shed door was laying on the ground and the contents were removed. Finally letting out a heavy breath, I felt relieved!

The sunset was a red blaze in the sky as I turned and walked away from the caretaker's shed. Walking back to the road, the church looked like the best place to get some rest. It was empty, the door was gone, the pews had been removed long ago, and everything had a thick layer of dust. Again, the remanence of other visitors was apparent in the cans, garbage, and graffiti. I hunkered down in a corner, as the night was cooling off quickly and I wanted to keep some heat. After walking in the sun most of the day, it felt much colder than it was. My eyes started to get heavy and I started to doze off. I awoke to movement outside, it sounded like feet walking. I rose and silently went over to the doorframe, but looking around, I saw nothing.

The moon had risen, and the stars twinkled in the night. I cautiously walked to the road and surveyed my surroundings. I felt it like a splash of cold water on my back! I turned around and froze in the middle of the road, stunned, as the dark-haired, five-year-old girl ran out from between the house and the church, giggling. She stopped at the side of the road and looked directly at me, her bright blue eyes fixed on my own. "Hello." That's all I could say! The girl started to walk my way, still staring at me, stopping five feet away. Looking up at me, she looked puzzled, blinking those big blue eyes at me. "You can see me? You can see me, can't you?" I nodded. "No one ever sees me, where are you from, what's your name!" "Susa.."

"Clo! Clo! Don't stay out too late." My head snapped to the right, and a man with black pants, a white shirt, and suspenders stood on the once empty porch, talking to the girl. Light poured out and flickered from the lantern inside the house. "Daddy, she sees me!" The man turned and looked directly at me. "You see us young lady?" the man asked with surprise. The man turned toward the door, "Mary! There's a young lady out here that can see us!" "Well, have her in, it's getting colder.," a woman's voice chimed from the house.

The smell of fresh bread caught my attention, and a small warm hand grasped mine and started to gently tug me in the direction of the house. ***Don't delve too deeply, you may not find your way back.*** The voice in my head was strong and commanding.

The man's voice overpowered my confusion, something familiar about it reminded me of my dream. Startled and staggering back a few steps from the intensity, I found myself looking down the empty road, abandoned, just the way I had found it. Startled and staggering back a few steps from the intensity, I found myself looking down the empty road. The moon was creeping into the night sky as fear surged through my entire being! I began turning and walking away with some haste.

"Well so much for shelter, I just keep walking! Not tired! I'm just gonna keep going! Camping is not my thing! At least there! Holy!!! Hah! Not a soul huh! Hah! Don't delve he says!"

Feeling like that was the best advice that I ever heard in my life, I spurred myself to get as far away from everything as I could. Walking was an easy task, I continued to think about that voice, "why does he seem so familiar" I was still talking out loud, which seemed to have become a habit since I left the graveyard and its patrons! *I don't need company THAT bad, God no!*

The chill of the night couldn't penetrate my thought as I moved on down the road, just the moon and starlight seemed to be all I needed. I didn't struggle to see, even though the moon was waning a little less than half. I didn't stumble on the occasional protruding stone, and my travel seemed absent of obstacles. I didn't feel fatigued, as I watched the moon work its way to its downward descent in front of me. *West, keep going west!* and as I thought it, another thought took its place.

"Help me," she said. Curly light brown hair, no older than fifteen. I could feel the mental connection waver in and out. *"Who are you?"* I asked, as the vision cleared, more details started to flood into my mind. *"My name is Missy, can you help?"* She was laying on a small cot in a room with drab light blue walls and barred windows.

"Where are you?" A metal door, white with an eight by eight window with metal mesh in the glass. *"The hospital, so tired!"* Electronic locking doors. *"Are you in jail?"* Security systems and cameras in every room. *"No, Mental hospital, too many drugs, can't think right."* A medium building, one story. Trying to get more detail, I asked, *"Where at?"*

The sign says Silver Wood Mental Hospital! *"I don't know, I can't remember, can't think…."* City lights, a pyramid, so many people, lights on the water, Mirage, The Bellagio! *She's in Vegas!* Making a small adjustment from the bootleg canyon hiking trail that I found to the river mountain powerline RD., I felt like two more hours or so ought to do the trick. I was making short work of an eight-hour jaunt through the boonies.

As luck would have it again, I had burned six hours of my jaunt in the right direction before I had a sense of direction! The scenery was greening up, and the smell of water was getting closer. An old sign reading "Clark County Wetlands Park" caught my attention, and with the rising sun, I was crossing a pretty swampy stretch of ground.

Knowing it was probably a bad idea to go helping a phantom vision, I couldn't shake the thought that within twenty-four hours of my hospital visit, my fate would surely be the same.

Dumped for dead in a canyon by an unknown assailant, ugh! I hope for my sake that I remain dead to that individual. Seems like I have an affinity for trouble, so I'm not too surprised at this point. And going to find more! God! I'm a piece of work, apparently.

With the area becoming more inhabited, I stuck to the woods as I worked my way north. *Hollywood Regional Park, not much further now!* As the patch of forest ended, the sudden change to suburbia was apparent. Houses littered the view as the sun started to make its move to the horizon. It seemed that I was lucky enough to be on the backside of the action here. About a hundred yards to the right was the start of a chain-link fence, and two hundred yards farther stood a large facility, the mercury switch lights starting to flicker with the oncoming dawn.

Well, here we go! Not being able to imagine why I was about to break, a perfect stranger out of a mental institute, or what made me think that I could for that matter.

Not scaling that fence. Looking at the fierce razor wire lining the top. *What! Do these people think this is Alcatraz or something!* Moving down the fence looking, and sure enough, *something has been digging!*

Under a large cropping of brush that had grown up against the fence was a fairly large hole. *Looks like maintenance has been slacking.* With a little effort, I made it through to the other side. Feeling like there was less security in this area, I sprinted as fast as I could down the fence on the backside of the building.

I stopped to catch my breath between two large air conditioning units. On the other side of them were two large vents secured on the inside of the facility. *Crap! Now how do I get in?* By the look of them, the vent grates were too sturdy to kick in, and the noise factor would not be good. At a loss, I sat down against the wall.

Closing my eyes, I thought, *think of something!* From the darkness behind my eyelids, I felt my consciousness shift, the wall became as thin as air, the boiler room behind me was as plain as day in my mind, and the maintenance office and the stairs, security keypad at the top, air ducts, rooms, lobby, bathrooms, guards, orderlies, med room, nurses, doctors sitting in their offices, room numbers, security cameras, wiring! *Rooms! 61, 62 ,64 yes!* In room 64, somehow, I could feel a sort of anomaly,

"Missy! Is that you? Get up!" The young girl raised her head and looked around groggily. **"I'm gonna try to help you get out of there, but you have to do what I tell you! Can you manage that?"** She gave a nod.

The room was fairly small with a security camera in the corner, positioned to see the entire room. *Maintenance IS slacking!* The room was in poor repair, and the bracket on the metal bed frame was loose. The security window in the door had a crack in it. The ventilation grate in the bathroom hadn't been serviced in a long time, and vibration had taken its toll. Room check was happening in three minutes and med pass in twenty-five, which didn't give much time for error!

"Missy, the bracket on the leg of your bed closest to the wall is loose, try to take it off and get back into bed. You got about three minutes." As I figured, the bolts were finger tight, and the bracket came off with no trouble! **"Pretend you are sleeping. The orderly is on his way there now."** The auto-lock on the door buzzed and a young man walked in the room, one earbud in, giving a quick look around and then he turned and headed back out the door. As soon as the door clicked shut, it was on!

"Slowly get up and go to the bathroom. Act tired! Once you get in there, try to pry the air vent open with that bracket." *Well, at least there are no security cameras in the bathroom! That would be unethical.* After about ten minutes, the grate was loose. **"Go in backward, I'll guide you! Try to put the grate back as best you can."** After a few turns and some easy declines and drops, she was in the maintenance area close to where I was waiting. *Four minutes left, I got to time this right.* Even with my shifted conciseness, I could feel my heart pounding! There were still Four maintenance guys down here, and all hell was about to break loose!

CHAPTER FIVE

Instant Outlaws

*O*ne minute! *"**Missy! Back up a little more, there will be a grate in the drop-down! When I tell you, jump down as hard as you can!!**"* "Code yellow! All available personnel proceed to the south wing! I repeat code yellow! All available personnel to the south wing!"

The four maintenance guys headed up the stairs and out the door. *"**Now!**"* With a crash, the grate broke downward under the girl's weight! *"**To your right is a tool room! There's a crowbar on the table! Hurry!**"*

The girl, finding the crowbar, looked around franticly! "Over here at the vent!" my consciousness crashed back, "Quick, pry the vent from the inside!!" I was kicking the vent as hard as I could as Missy pried from the other side! Bang! The large vent plate broke loose and hit the floor!

Dragging the girl through the hole, she looked at me and started to tear up. "Thank you so much!" "Thank me later! Run!!!" Half a second later, we were sprinting across the divide between us and freedom! Hitting the fence hard and then to the ground crawling through the hole! Missy squeezing through when yells emanated from the outside of the building! Stop!!! There she goes! That way! And back to a full sprint again, "Come on we gotta move!!!"

We made our more than hasty retreat to the woods, entering the wood line in no quiet fashion. We were making some ground on our pursuers but had no time to stop and chat. She was fast and keeping up well, and with the meds wearing off, she picked up speed and dexterity by the minute it seemed.

Going north, we made some distance in a short time, but the run was starting to catch up to us. Missy was starting to breathe heavily, and the pace had slowed, but at least we were starting to go downhill now.

The heat was rising as the sun started to climb, and the moisture of the oncoming wetlands that I had gone through earlier was building humidity quickly. Sweat started to run down my face and my clothes were starting to stick, but it would worse before it got better.

We had a fast and steady pace going now, and again, we were covering some ground. *I can't believe we pulled that off!* Feeling a little confused but having much greater respect for my current condition. *Condition? Is it a condition? I'm definitely NOT imagining things!* And after that thought, I had a new and growing confidence about my…"*condition.*"

Our pace was slowing a bit, as the overgrowth had gotten much thicker, and it was harder to keep a steady pace. We were still moving right along, everything seemed fine minus the buzzing that was starting to get louder in my ears, which was getting annoying. Then, a sudden feeling of anxiety spread through my body.

"Missy, I'm getting a bad feeling." My words were cut short by her scream, "OUCH!" as she slapped the side of her neck! *Oh my god, she found the buzzing!* "BEES!!! Run!!"

Panic struck, and again we were running as fast as we possibly could! Looking back over my shoulder, Missy was gaining on me quick, and behind her, a monster swarm was gaining on her!

The look on her face was pure rage while we hurtled over rocks and dead trees, and the look on mine must have been pure fear! *No water nowhere to hide!* the monster swarm was like nothing I had ever seen, it was fast! The mass had tendrils that reached out trying to get around us and push us toward the center. *What is that thing?*

Two seconds later another scream, "OUCH!!!!!" Glancing over my shoulder again, I saw that Missy had stopped and was facing the oncoming mass! "Missy NOOOOO!!!" *What am I supposed to do!* Feeling my heart pound hard in my chest as time seemed to come to a stop, *Oh god, that's too many! They're gonna kill her!* Tripping hard on a downed log, feeling helpless as gravity took me backward to the ground. *I'll never make it to her in time!* Thud! Hitting the ground hard. The buzz stopped so abruptly I wondered if the fall had damaged my hearing. *What the…* "Missy? Are you okay?" Sobbing. "Are you hurt?" More sobbing!

I managed to get back on my feet in a hurry, not quite understanding what just happened. Missy was hunched over with her face in her hands. She sobbed, "All I wanted is for them to stop! I didn't want to cut their little threads! It makes me so sad!" The bee swarm lay scattered across the ground in thick-clumped piles surrounding here, but none were closer than two feet from the girl. *She killed them all! I thought she was a goner!*

The stings were already swelling up badly, I felt really sorry for this poor girl, she had really been through the wringer! Somehow, I knew her story but wasn't about to bring it up to myself. We needed rest and maybe a change of clothes. *I'm not camping out for the rest of my life, in fact, I'm tired of the great outdoors completely for the moment!*

Like a compass, with that thought, my senses queued up a direction, along with distance, about a half a mile to the nearest town. Also, a mental grid of the forest and surrounding area. These strange mental issues were continuing to increase, becoming more and more detailed every time they happened, all of these incidents were so bizarre. I was sure there must be something seriously wrong with me, but finding Missy made me think that I was not the only one, and as I collected up the still slightly sobbing girl, I had felt just a little less alone.

After walking for short while, I began to hear the movement of cars and the sound of the city in the distance. It seemed that we had been moving fast, which didn't bother me in the slightest. Emerging out of the forest we found ourselves on a fairly steep embankment with a weed fence for a separator. Down the bank was the hardtop, and on the other side of the road was a motel. Just in time, as the street lights started to pop on.

The day was spent as the sun cast a red sky as far as the eye could see. Taking a look at Missy, she was just a little too young to be my sister and looked slightly too old to be my daughter, unless I had her young! *God forbid!* But then I really had no idea how old I really was, maybe I was just being kind to myself. *Well daughter it is!* Turning to Missy, "You're gonna be my daughter, okay!" Missys' eyes widened, and noded as we make our way to the motel.

Cautiously making our way across the road and to the motel, the flashing neon on the sunrise motel sign cast a sickly green and yellow glow to the steadily darkening surroundings. Before we reached the door, we could hear the tv blaring in the lobby with no need of heightened senses.

An elderly lady sat at the front desk, and behind her, the tv on the wall mount is blaring out the evening news. "How can I help you dears this evening?" "The weather for this evening will be a balmy seventy-eight degrees, with light cloud cover in the morning." "We would like a room for the night!"

"We have room 308 available, is that okay?" Glancing down the line of doors outside, 308 looked to be almost at the end of the motel. "Yes! We will take it." "That will be sixty-five dollars, please." After shelling out the money, I grabbed the key and headed for the door.

"Breaking news alert, authorities are conducting a search for two young women, Missy Loren, age fifteen, escaped from the Silver Birch Mental Institution last night and is still at large, the individual is highly unstable and may be dangerous. The other female is a Jane Doe who left the Boulder City Hospital, against doctor's orders and…"

"Thank you dears, have a nice stay." Heading out the door, *stay calm just keep walking, nothing going on here, just keeeeep walking!* Feeling my heart slamming blood into my ears.

Missy and I headed for room 308, I could hear her increased breathing and an occasional sob. I could tell she was terrified. "They're gonna catch us, aren't they?" Fumbling with the key in the lock, "Not if I can help it, Missy!" But at that point, I was questioning my skill as a fugitive. "Get a shower and then we will make some type of plan as to what we do next," I said, and Missy nodded and headed for the bathroom with haste. As the shower kicked on, I flopped down on one of the two twin beds and stared at the newly applied cream-colored texture paint overlaying the sheetrock. *Make a plan huh! And what plan would that be? Keep running like hell? Live in the boonies? Ugh!*

My energy started to pick up after Missy finished with her shower. She came out drying her hair and got a change of clothes; they were a little bit big but clean. Now it was my turn, moving as fast as possible, jumping in the shower, and hurrying like the devil was at the door, I cleaned the days of dirt and sweat off. Before I was done drying, I could hear sirens, they seemed to be very far away, my senses told me about six miles.

"Yes, that's right, they are coming for you!" The man's voice in my head was strong. I let out a squeal and almost panicked. I threw on my clothes.

"Who are you? I know you can hear me!" **"My name is Sylus, and I am aware of your predicament! I will be there in three minutes, be ready, you don't have much time!"**

"Missy! We are leaving!" *What the hell do I mean we are leaving. Just gonna up and run off with the voice in my head huh!* Senses peaked, *those sirens are getting closer, about 3.5 miles now! Yep! It's happening!* Like clockwork, I heard the low rumble of a car pull up right in front of the door!

Peeking out the window, *the voice in my head drives an '86 Monte Carlo SS huh! Good taste! What the hell is wrong with me, this is not a time for joking!* The dark blue Monte Carlo just sat there, shining like a showroom in the neon. The driver was not visible through the dark tinted windows. I took the lead out the door as the driver's side window lowered. Keeping my distance a bit, I looked in the window at the dark curly-haired man sitting in the driver's seat. He looked out at me with a half-smile, "I'm Sylus, you ladies look as if you could use some help."

"Um, yes we could." My voice was shaky. I just stood there staring at him.

His voice was definitely the voice I had heard in my head several times. He looked over his shoulder at the road. "I would have preferred to have a more formal introduction, but I think we had best be going now, I really don't wanna make a scene." He was right, I could hear the sirens heading in our direction. "Come on Missy, get in."

We jumped in the back and were on the road before I had time to get my seat belt fastened. Looking out of my window, I could see the old lady at the desk peering out the motel lobby window. *That old biddy turned us in!* Shaking off the anger, I turned back to the driver, who looked back at us through the rear-view mirror.

"Sorry if I startled you ladies, and I will be happy to answer all your questions when we get you to safety." I felt a surge of relief, someone had answers. I had this sense of traveling a great distance, everything seemed jumpy the scenery seemed to change before my eyes. It reminded me of a kaleidoscope, but the pieces kept changing. The world seemed mirrored and warped somehow. *Fatigue must be getting to me, I can't even see straight. And this guy! He has answers, does he?* I couldn't think of any reasonable answer to the things that had transpired over the last few days. Everything was beyond reason. At this point, even a bad answer was better than what I had.

The lights came on in a large concrete parking garage. The car rumbled to a stop. Sylus, shutting off the car, let out a sigh. "You should be safe now, please come in." Exiting the car, I extended my senses to get an idea as to where we were. To my surprise I got nothing, it was as if we weren't anywhere. I could hear the sound of classical music coming from somewhere in the house. Sylus exited the car and opened the door for me, gesturing towards the stairs leading out of the parking garage.

The parking garage was large, about ten feet high with square concrete columns. Several other vehicles were parked, including a mean-looking Humvee. *Man, this guy must be loaded.*

As we headed up the stairs to the door, we passed a large metal divider that I assumed was probably a large shop. I started to feel a feeling of familiarity again. Going through the door and into the hallway, my boots made a soft tapping sound on the red granite tiles on the floor. *And wall paint the color of red velvet cake! Imagine that!* We walked down the hallway toward the door at the end. The beautifully carved dark hardwood door matched the trim of the rest of the hallway. Sylus opened the door and made a gesture to enter. "Make yourselves comfortable, we have a lot to talk about."

We entered the softly lit office. It had several comfortable-looking chairs along the walls and two in front of a large desk. A television on a wall mount was showing the news, and again, it seemed we had become the center of attention in the greater Las Vegas area. As I watched, I heard, "Police are on the lookout for two women in connection a recent breakout and vandalization of Silver Oaks Mental Institution, the suspects were last seen heading northbound on state route 95," and there I was. *Oh, wonderful, they got me on camera somewhere!*

"The suspects were last seen driving a white Town and Country minivan. Confusion struck me, *A minivan? What minivan?* I looked at our rescuer questioningly. "Well, it appears that they got some of their facts wrong now doesn't it?" he said with a grin. *How do you mistake a muscle car for a minivan? That's just nonsense in itself!* Our host clicked the remote and the tv went silent.

Along the walls, there were also some glass display cases with some antique swords, helmets, armor, and other odd-looking items. We took a seat in the two red velvet upholstered chairs in front of the desk as our host took a seat in the large high back chair behind the desk. "Well, then." Sylus looked up from his desk after a glance at some papers that sat there. "So now for that more formal introduction, I'm Sylus, and you are Susan and Missy." We nodded. "I suppose you feel like Alice falling down the rabbit hole at the moment, forgive my quotes."

"So, where to begin." I was aquiver with anticipation, a sense of excitement and urgency overwhelmed me! "As you both have figured out, you are in possession of some very strange and unique talents, which you will be surprised to know is not as uncommon as you might think. These gifts are inherent to humankind, but as time progressed, people lost the abilities, save a few. Heroes of times past, people with great skill in certain areas. But the secrets of their success are well kept. People who keep the secret become kings, and people who show the world get crucified."

"The nature of things does not like the unknowing to see the spectacular, it always has consequences. Sometimes, people who have been in a traumatic event are able to deal with more than most, our willingness to accept what is real is the key to reality. Most do not accept the real, so their scope is much smaller. This is part of the reality we call the Magendra."

"The Magendra encompasses reality and the rules of reality, dimensions, energy, matter, the material, and the immaterial. The people that live in this reality live a higher existence, the world inside of the world, a realm inside of a realm."

"Everything is real, but it has been hidden from view for the protection of all, the government knows about it. The CIA, FBI, NSA, and all the rest have been trying to exploit our kind for centuries and have succeeded in some instances. So, again, forgive me, but the rabbit hole is deep, and you are on your way to see just how far it goes. Not that you had a choice in the matter, but here you are!" He paused, looking at us, waiting for a response.

My head was spinning, it sounded so far-fetched, but I couldn't prove different, the events leading to this point were indeed extraordinary. "So, what is your part in all this? Why have you been helping us? And believe me, I'm grateful."

He smiled. "I couldn't in good conscience let you get yourself locked up and tested like some lab rat because you're special, plus I run a program that deals with incidents of supernatural nature. We are called sentinels, for lack of a better word. We deal with events that the normal world is not equipped to deal with. My main focus is to train those who are special, teach them to fit into the world we know and the world we are from, and offer them a chance to have a life."

Getting my head wrapped around what I was just told was a bit of a task, *a life, that's something I don't have or at least know of. And training, for what! God, I don't even know what to think about that!* But I was thinking, and I knew curiosity would win. "What sort of training?" I asked. Sylus chuckled, a large grin spreading across his face; he seemed to glow with the idea.

"Training of the exceptional kind Susan, purely exceptional! And since we are on the subject, let me show you some of the house and to your rooms. Feel free to look around, but use caution, some places of the house can be dangerous, and it is very large. You may want to train up a bit before venturing too far." Sylus walked to the door and motioned for us to follow.

As we were walking down the hall, Sylus continued, "As I was saying about the abilities being inherent to everyone, for example, if someone is looking at you, most people will sense it and look back, its considered instinct, and people don't think about it much because of how common it seems but in fact its...."

My attention went to a plant sitting on an end table in the hall as we were walking by.

What is it, I've never seen anything like it, I swear I just saw it move. I turned to the plant. It was a vine of some sort, as I got closer one of the vines reached out toward me, in the center of the plant it looked like some type of leafy buds, six of them, and they were all turned as if looking at me. The iridescent purple, blue, and green of the plant was very attractive, and it seemed to move in the light.

In front of the plant, there was a small gold plaque that read "Deamonium Comedere Vinea." *Wow, that is amazing!* I put out my hand, and the small plant wrapped one viny tendril around the end of my finger as the bulb heads all leaned slightly forward.

"Susan, be very careful with her, she can very temperamental!" "What in the world is it! It's amazing!" He pointed at the plaque. "It says 'Demon Eating Vine' in Latin, I just call her Audrey, she has a temper."

Demon Eating Vine! so pretty, and it seems quite friendly to me. I gently removed the little vine from the end of my finger and turned back to Sylus and began to follow again. The hall split four ways, and our host led us to the right, down the hallway.

There were several doors on each side of the hall; he stopped at the first and pointed at the mark carved into the door. "Missy, this is your room, and Susan, yours on the other side of the hall." He opened the door, and the room was large, lavishly furnished with a king-size bed with a canopy, a huge dresser with a mirror, a large desk, a full stone tile bathroom complete with a walk-in shower, and a jacuzzi. *Oh, my sweet lord! These are our rooms! I won't know what to do with myself!*

I was thinking about a real night's sleep for a change! *Now, this is the kind of survival that I'm interested in!* Sylus turned to Missy, "Young lady, you look like you need some rest, why don't you get comfortable, and we will get you for dinner?" Missy was eyeing the bed; the poor girl had been moving nonstop since I retrieved her from that horrible facility. *Man, that really ticks me off, what those people did to that poor girl!*

Now that I had time and wasn't running for my life, the annoyance of past events came to the top, and the presence of my temper became more evident. *I do have a temper now don't I? I suppose not having a memory about yourself could be a dangerous thing, I'm gonna have to watch out for that.*

Missy let out a quiet, "Thank you." I could see the tear of relief welling up in her eyes as she surveyed the beautiful room. "All right then, Susan, you can come with me if you want, and I'll show you some more of this facility. We will let Missy get some well-deserved rest."

Chapter Six

Bolt

Leaving Missy in her room, Sylus, turned back up the hall and continued. "There are a few key things that you should think about. First of all, your abilities are only limited to what you can accept; for instance, some people train for years to build enough confidence in themselves to perform a task. They have always been physically and mentally able to do the task, but it all boils down to if you believe that you are able, the more you feel that it's possible for you to succeed, the better the success will be."

"The more you believe in your reality the more real it becomes. Secondly, every action you make, every feat you do, creates a soft ripple that flows out and affects everything and everyone around you. Kind of like a pebble in still water, but if the action is too powerful and unreal, it will bounce back to the source and that can be really bad."

"Situations involving the unaware will increase the chance of backfire exponentially."

He had turned left and was walking past laboratories and storerooms with sliding glass doors, filled with all manners of things. *This place is massive!*

He turned again to the right. This hallway appeared to be sided with painted metal. There were several short hallways going left and right leading to sturdy steel doors with keypads attached to them. Sylus took the second hallway to the left and hit the green button on the keypad.

Before the door started to slide open, my ears could pick up a faint hum, and the hair on my arms started to stand up from static. As the door swished open, the energy coming from the room was overwhelming, it looked like a computer lab with multiple large monitors and servers. The rest of the room looked like some kind of science lab with all manner of electronics-related equipment. In the center sitting in a chair was a kid with a fancy VR headset making motions in the air. Sylus stared at him for a moment. "Bolt." The boy just kept moving his hands through the air. "BOLT!" The boy snatched the headset off and jumped out of his chair.

"Hi Sylus, what's up!" He had a big smile on his face like someone who just got caught with his hand in the cookie jar. "Bolt, I would like you to meet our new guest, this is Susan, Susan this is Bolt. He has an affinity for electric and energy types like a human lightning rod."

Bolt looked at me still smiling as the VR goggles crept slowly around to his back, hidden from view.

"Hi Susan, I'm Bolt." The kid was only about thirteen or fourteen, grinning that sheepish grin, blushing a little. "You got to forgive Bolt, he doesn't get out much. But that's more his choice, isn't it Bolt?" Bolt looked down at his feet. "Well, it's scary out there Sylus, I get nervous."

"I hear ya!" Sylus retorted, "I'm gonna be out for a while, so don't break anything while I'm gone, okay?" Bolt nodded "And Bolt! Try not to terrify our new guests will ya?" "I'll do my best Sylus." As we turned and headed for the door, I glanced back and saw that Bolt was headed back to his chair, watching us intently as the VR goggles started creeping back out from behind him.

Suddenly, Sylus spun around fast enough that I jumped. Bolt sprung up from his half squat, the rollers on the chair he had almost been sitting in clattered across the floor, and at the same time, a huge CRACK, sparks flew around the room as a bolt of electricity bounced from electrical device to electrical device, and ended as abruptly as it had started.

"Aw Sylus! Why would you do that! It's gonna take me hours to fix all that!"

Sylus put his hands on his hips and cocked his head to the side. "I think you should be practicing your control instead of playing on that VR all the time!" "Try not to break anything else will ya!"

Bolt was already whining and mumbling as we left the room he set to work on the fried electronics.

As I ran the event through my head, the more bizarre it seemed. I was starting to get used to strange anomalies, and I was strangely fine with it. After leaving, we walked down the hall to the end where another large steel door stood. Reaching it, Sylus pushed the button on the keypad, the door opened, and we walked in. This room was empty, and the walls were solid stone, light blue with purple tints, but I had no idea what type.

"This is the practice room. It's a safe place to explore your abilities without incident. To wrap up my explanation of the Magendra as best I can, every fiction movie that you have ever watched has some basis of truth, and they all exist in the Magendra. I like to use movies because I love them, and quote them more than I probably should." He paused, looking at me as I considered what he was saying.

"So, what you are saying is that anything is possible?" "Pretty much! It's possible and probable that if you can imagine it, it exists somewhere in the Magendra." Sylus turned a bit, reached into the pocket of his black cargo pants, and produced a baseball. I was pretty sure that that pocket had been empty just a moment ago.

"Well let's see what you can do, shall we? Throw this as fast as you can at that wall."

He tossed me the ball. *All right then.* I wound up and threw the ball with all the strength that I could muster, the ball sped across the room, hitting the wall with a thud. Sylus started to walk over to pick up the ball.

"Good! That was about fifty miles per hour. That was a good throw!" he said. He picked up the ball and turned to me. "This time, reach out with your awareness and feel the distance, then when you throw, squeeze the space, and the ball will go faster." He tossed the ball back to me. *Okay, feel the space and squeeze it!*

I reached out with my senses and could feel the distance. It felt real to me, tangible, almost solid like the ball I held in my hand. I wound up and, *Now squeeze!* The ball hit the wall with a loud crack, the threads snapped, and it left a white spot on the wall from where the leather from the ball was removed from the impact. The ball dropped to the ground and disappeared. I stared, dumbfounded at where the ball should have been.

"Now that was really amazing," Sylus said. "That ball was moving at nearly 600 miles per hour! That is certainly an improvement, don't you think?" I looked back at Sylus, then sudden shock hit me.

There he was looking at the ball in his hand, examining the damage. He rubbed his hand over the ball then handed it back to me. It was perfect, no visible damage, and the ball looked new. "You can come here and practice as much as you like."

"Feel free to enjoy the house, I have to get some dinner ready." He smiled. "Can you find your way back okay" I nodded and smiled back. Sylus walked out the door, and the door slid shut behind him. I stood there for a while, staring at the baseball in my hand. *That was by far the craziest thing I had ever seen, Humm I wonder! What happens if I stretch the distance a bit?*

I wound up, threw the ball as hard as I could, and stretched the distance. The ball flew all of three feet and plopped onto the ground. *Well, that makes sense!* **Just reach out and pick it up, Susan. Reach THROUGH the space.** Sylus's voice entered my mind, Warm and familiar. *God, this guy!*

I reached out using my awareness, and at the same time I reached my hand out, I could feel my hand wrap around the ball. I pulled it back through the space. The feeling of the ball still remained in my hand. And it was there! Excitement hit me like a wave. I stifled some choice metaphors and the urge to dance around.

Nope! Not gonna make a fool of myself, but that was bar none the most amazing thing I can remember ever doing! Which wasn't much. *Well, I think I'm done here!* I turned and headed toward the door.

I don't feel like I have a problem anymore, I'm a believer. My heart still pounded with excitement, and the smile on my face threatened to become permanent. *Let's just see what else is around here, this place is amazing!*

I went to another door along the hallway and pushed the button; the door breezed open, revealing a room full of all sorts of inanimate materials, the floor was sand and stone and dirt, there were patches of mud and piles of steel, charcoal, wood, and cloth. It was just a mess of material with no organization.

What a strange room, there must be a thousand materials in here! I could sense that there was more than that, so much clutter that it made my head hurt. *Nope, none of that for me today, I'll find something else to do.* Leaving the room, I decided to go back the way I came and get a closer look at some of the many rooms I passed on my way to the training room. As I walked, I was thinking about the mental connection that Sylus and I had. I seemed to have it with Missy for a time as well, but now her mind had gone quiet or at least our connection had.

Reaching out with my senses. *Man, this place is huge, I can't get any idea of where it's located though, it's like it's nowhere!* In no time, I was back to the rooms with the sliding glass doors. I pressed the button, and the door opened with a swish.

The room was full of lighted glass display cases, each housing a set of oddities. It was curated similar to a museum. Light bounced off from stone wood and steel, and it was beautiful. There were glass cases in the center of the room, too- the type you might see in a jewelry store.

One case that was closest to me held a beautifully decorated blunderbuss, complete with a matching embossed leather shot pouch, with five types of shot also displayed as well. The first type was what appeared to be steel ball bearings about the size of marbles and a pile of coarse green sand, another was a blue ball with black stripes giving it a marbled look, then some crystal-looking material and a pile of material looking like straw.

This is strange. It looks odd, something about this stuff is different!! It was giving me a feeling like you would feel if you were standing next to a nuclear warhead. It made me nervous.

As I looked around the room, my senses were heightened. Every single thing in this room was either powerful or dangerous or both. Even the small hand-carved figurines seemed to yell out, "Touch me if you dare!" Works of art from wall to wall seemed to seep power.

After a good look around, I decided to go back to my room, only stopping for a moment to visit with my new plant friend in the hallway before getting to my room.

When I got to the room, I opened the door and stepped inside. The room was large enough, furnished with a king-sized bed, and had ample space. It also had a large desk made of dark hardwood. The walls were painted dark forest green. The sheets and décor matched. Closing the door behind me, I laid down on the bed; it was soft and it felt as if it was about to consume me. I just laid there for a while staring at the ceiling, all of the events for the past few days came flooding back to me making my head spin even more. I was tired and it felt good to lie there and relax for a while. I closed my eyes, feeling myself slipping away.

Knock! knock! there was a rap and the door. I woke up with the start, "Yes?" "Dinner is ready if you would like to join us." Sylus's voice chimed from the other side of the door. *Now, food is worth getting up for.*

CHAPTER SEVEN

Dinner and a Story

Opening the door, I greeted Sylus with a nod, as we both started walking down the hall, I could already smell the food. At the intersection of the hall, he turned to the right. The large dining hall was well lit, and a large chandelier hung over the top of the massive table.

The smell of roast filled the room. Large silver platters of food covered the table. Mashed potatoes, corn, freshly-baked bread, and other trimmings beckoned me. My stomach growled furiously, *it all looks so good, I am so hungry!*

Sylus pulled out a chair for me at the end of the table. I took my seat, waiting as patiently as possible. Our host sat down at the other end of the table, and with a flourish, he exclaimed, "Enjoy!"

Bolt and Missy sat next to each other talking quietly. Their plates were already filled, but they waited patiently for everybody else to get comfortable. I loaded my plate as politely as I could. We all began to eat. About halfway through the meal, Sylus look at Missy.

"Would you be so kind as to tell us a little bit about yourself, Missy?" Missy looked up from her food. "What would you like to know?" she asked. "Well just tell us a little bit about yourself and how you managed to get put into that institution?" Missy looked down at her plate for a moment, "I can't remember too much of it." she said. "I think I was in there for a very long time. My parents were killed. And after that, I ended up in the institution."

At that point, I was feeling really bad for her. "What happened to them, Missy?" I asked.

Somehow, I already knew what the response would be. "They were shot by a robber." "Did they capture him?" I asked. "No, he just died, they said he walked into the yard and keeled over dead. After that, they took me and put me in the institution."

There was a pause of silence, Sylus's looked up from his plate. "We're certainly glad to have you with us here now Missy." After a few moments, Sylus turned to me. "Is there anything that you can recall about your situation, Susan?" Sylus asked. "Nope, I got nothing, just probably what you already know. I woke up in the desert, with hardly anything to my name, and, really, I don't even have one of those. I can't remember who I am or where I came from."

Sylus looked down for a moment; it looked like he was taking a minute to contemplate the conversation. "How was it that you came to find out about our situation, Sylus?" I questioned. "You were not too hard to find, with you plastered all over the news. I knew something was up when they started throwing a fit about a Jane Doe escaping from a hospital. And lucky for us, you found Missy, as they had her tucked away, very secretively. There is a good chance that they'll start a big stink!"

Sylus let out a sigh of relief and sat back in his chair. "I'm just happy that everybody is safe now, that's the most important thing. I took the liberty of getting some extra clothes put in your room for you, if there's anything else that you need, feel free to ask. I'm sure you ladies can use some rest after everything that you've been through, and we can continue in the morning."

Sylus got up from the table and walked through the doors, leaving us with the piles of food still sitting on the table. We all told him goodnight. *Now back to the important stuff, having a decent meal for a change.* I continued to eat until I was content. My stomach was full, and my mind, after a long time, had finally come to ease, and I was relaxed. Missy and Bolt appeared to be getting along very well; they sat at the table and giggled amongst themselves. I was happy to see that she had found someone with whom she could relate.

She didn't seem like the same girl anymore after the drugs were all out of her system. She was happy, smiling, and acting like any girl her age. I decided to let them be, as they seemed to be enjoying themselves. I headed back to my room, curious to see what kind of extra clothing was left for me.

He took the liberty of getting extra clothes for me, did he, I'm certainly not going to say no to that. Getting back to my room, I felt right at home. That's probably because I didn't have a home to remember feeling anything about. This one suited me just fine. Going over to the closet in my room, I opened the door and took a look in, and I saw that the closet was full. There were jeans, shirts, and even some dresses. There were also a pair of leather pants, a leather shirt, and a heavy black leather jacket. Oddly enough, something about these items was different, as there seemed to be energy running through them.

Whoa! Those look tough! Now that's the kind of gear I needed when I was running for my life! I couldn't help myself, I took the leather gear out of the closet and laid it on the bed.

Yeah! I'm gonna wear them!

I put on the leather pants and shirt; they were more comfortable than they looked. They fit perfectly, the clothing seemed to wrap and form itself to my body. I had never felt anything that fit so perfectly. After wearing them for a while, I decided to go to bed. Rummaging through the closet, I found some comfortable sweatpants and a loose shirt. Swapping out my leathers, I set them on the cedar chest at the end of my bed. I slept soundly.

Knock, knock! I woke up. Bolt's voice on the other side of the door chimed out, "Breakfast!" and then he was gone. Getting out of my nightclothes, I changed back into those wonderful leathers. They fit with immense comfort. *I don't know why anybody would want to wear anything else!*

I went directly to the dining room. As before, the table was full of all manner of food- pancakes, French toast, eggs, sausage, and fruit toppings. It was all so appealing. Again, I sat down and ate like I was starving. **Susan, could you come to my office when you get a moment!**

Sylus's voice in my head didn't startle me this time; it was like I could feel the phone ring before his voice popped into my head. *Oh, I'm getting good at this now, can't surprise me anymore.* Proud of myself, I finished eating and headed out to the office.

Before I reached the office, I could sense two people talking, one was Sylus and the other was someone that I did not know. My accelerated hearing kicked in almost automatically. "Are you sure you want to let someone so new do that Sylus?" "I have full confidence in Susan's abilities, if she feels she is up for the task, I will be the first to allow her to do it."

"You're the boss Sylus, I just want to impress on you that I believe this is connected to something big." "Thank you for your concern, Thomas, I'm sure we can get this taken care of in a quick and efficient manner." I got to the door and reached to knock, "Come in Susan, no need to knock." Behind the door, she heard Thomas gasp. "What the!"

I felt his presence disappear altogether. I turned the knob on the door and entered. I tried with all my might to keep the smile from my face as our eyes met, all of that talk of confidence in my ability and choices had definitely hit a nerve, a good one. He smiled a large grin, and it was my undoing, as a smile broke through onto my face and my cheeks were set on fire.

Oh damn, I have got to look like I have a sunburn, my face is on fire! Seeing my distress, Sylus advanced the subject. "I see you have found your fighting leathers, what do you think of them?" "They're super comfy." "Good, I'm glad you like them. They can be very useful, I designed them myself! They're one of a kind."

Sylus looked down at the papers on his desk. "As you have probably figured out, I have an errand that I need someone to attend to if you feel up for some excitement." He looked at me with a questioning look.

"There has been a disturbance that needs looking into, and I thought you might want to help me out with it. That is entirely up to you. No pressure." He said it in a way that I didn't feel pressured, but my rising curiosity was getting the best of me.

He knows I can't resist, of course, I wanna do something. God, I don't even know what I'm doing yet and I'm all in! probably not my smartest move, but I can't just sit here and do nothing for the rest of my life. I do have to admit, it's not a hard life at this point, though! Well, no sense in beating around the bush!

"Of course, I'm interested. From what that fellow was saying it sounds important. By the way, where did he go? He was just in here a moment ago?" "He didn't notice that you were there, Thomas is a little skittish most of the time, he doesn't like to be surprised, it was good for him! That will take 'Mr. I'm So Sneaky' down a cog!" Sylus was chuckling, but he really didn't answer my question, Thomas had definitely dematerialized before I came in the room.

You just keep your secrets then, I WILL figure it all out eventually! "So, what are we doing then?" I asked. "As I was saying, there has been a disturbance in one of the museums belonging to one of our patrons, the silent alarm went off a little while ago, and the intrusion needs to be investigated. Due to the nature of the facility and the nature of our patron, we are to discretely take care of the situation without the authorities getting involved."

"I suppose I can go in and take a look, what should I do if I find something?" That was really the question, what if I ran into the intruder, what was I gonna do, immediately my thoughts went back to the exercise with the baseball. *I wouldn't want to be on the receiving end of that!*

"Capture if you can, but if necessary, use any amount of force you need," Sylus said,

"Your safety is the highest priority!" Sylus got up and walked over to the wall next to one of the displays, making some motion with his hand, a section of the wall moved aside producing a safe, he gingerly punched in the code, and the safe opened with a beep.

"You will be needing a little something for your endeavor." He produced a wide thin box from the safe and set it on top of the papers that were laid out across the large desk. The wooden case was about three and a half feet long by two feet wide, of polished red lacquer, and had two tough-looking metal clasps holding it shut.

Sylus unlocked the clasps and opened the lid, revealing that the container had a variety of expensive and dangerous-looking knives, a bowie, a switchblade, a tanto, and even a Japanese wakizashi. They all looked to be handcrafted and somehow old, despite their perfectly new appearance. "Go ahead and pick one, they are all wonderful blades."

As I looked over the organization of shiny blades, a snaking blade of folded damasks caught my eye, as the blade looked deadly sharp. The knife was a little longer than some, with a large brass cross guard, a black leather-wrapped handle with a brass pommel. The hilt of the curvy dagger was fairly plain, the brass was finely polished, but, in comparison to the blade with its swirling steel and incandescent shimmer, the rest seemed plain. I pointed. "That one is nice."

Sylus gently removed the Kris from the case and handed it to me. He went back over to the safe and produced a sheath with a chest harness. It was equipped with a mag light and several pouches. He brought it over to me, and I gently slid the Kris into the sheath. Sylus looked at me for a moment.

"There that should do it, don't you think?" I put on the harness and replaced my leather jacket over top. "I don't know what you will run into so be careful, and don't hesitate to use force if you are in danger." I felt as ready as I was going to get.

"So where are we going? Are we taking the car?" Actually, I was hoping he would say the hummer. "No," he said. "I have a much faster way, follow me." Leaving the case sitting on the desk, he led me out of the office. This time, we went to the right and down the hall, where he then turned right again.

"All you have to do is evict the intruder and collect all the info you can in the process, and when you're finished with that, just give me a yell and I'll come to pick you up. I'm going to stay on this side and make sure nothing gets out, as far as the authorities go, this never happened. Like I said, we want these issues to stay contained."

About halfway down the hall, Sylus stopped at a door and opened it. The room was completely empty, and the walls and floor were all painted white. Sylus looked at me. "Get ready. This is going to feel really funny! You may wanna go at a bit of a run if you're nervous!" Feeling a bit goofy, I took his advice. Taking a few steps back I made a run at the door. *I feel like such an idiot…*

My thought was cut off by the urge to scream, as I bounded through the frame of the door. I felt like a long jumper that had just launched themselves, but instead of twenty feet, this jump was much faster and much farther. It was over so quickly that the scream that had started ended up just a gasp as my feet slammed down in the grass beside a large empty parking lot. *Holy Crap! That is super intense!*

As the vertigo from the experience subsided, the change of scenery was a bit of a shock as well. The sandy sparse landscape of Nevada had been replaced with rolling mountains and dense forest. The overcast, early September sky threatened rain, and humidity hung heavy in the air.

Stepping out into the empty parking lot, I surveyed my new surroundings. The sign in front of the museum read "World Museum of Ancient War." *That has the potential to be problematic, too late to change my mind now I guess.* I started toward the glass double doors, and I already could feel where the intruders were and there were five of them.

The museum was a big one; it was multi-floor but there was only one floor above ground, and the other two floors were below the ground. Entering the building, I saw suits of armor lined both sides of the main hallway at the entrance. The main hallway led to an open, hexagonal lounge area with large skylights, and vending stands were closed and locked up in the center of the room.

From here there were five directions you could go, each to a different exhibit. There was a huge compass made from tile on the floor that was accurate; each passage corresponded with a point of the compass. It was a beautiful piece of art, the contrast of the brown, grey, and bronze-colored tile gave it a rustic but elegant look.

The lighting was on, and the place looked open for business. My heightened senses told me that the compass direction that I needed was to the west. In the second hall on the left, the hall was marked with an exhibit list called, "Ancient Ranged Weapons and Siege Machines."

Oh, that's just lovely! I crept down the hall, as silently as I possibly could. I could sense two life forms in the display room marked Eastern Native American. The exhibit room's large opening without a door was on my right, and getting closer, I could hear the slight sound of movement on the carpeted floor. My hearing was peaked, and like an animal, I could triangulate the exact location of the sound coming from the back right corner of the exhibit room.

Getting to the edge of the entrance, I carefully took a peek around the corner. The fluorescent lighting cast a glow off the lit display cases arranged around the center of the room, along with the numerous wall exhibits. The room had gone quiet, and the hum of the lighting was the only sound.

C H A P T E R   E I G H T
Save the Pieces

I could still feel the intruders in the room and the sense of something else. *I'm being watched, do they know I'm here?* I got down low and sipped behind the nearest case. It was about three and a half feet tall and about four feet from the wall. I had to crouch pretty low to stay concealed. Looking through the glass case, I could see a distorted figure slip up on top of one of the cases on the other side of the room as quiet as death. I could tell it was on top of the floor case on all fours, but I couldn't determine who or what it was.

I gotta know what I'm up against, okay Susan! What exactly are you gonna do, what's the plan?. Slow! Go slow! Moving up slowly to take a look, my adrenaline started pumping, my blood seemed to be on fire! *Oh boy! Here we go!*

I knew I had to be ready, as I had a bad feeling that this was not going to go smoothly! Reaching inside of my jacket, I wrapped my hand around the hilt of the Kris as my head raised above the counter, just far enough that I could get a look. The person perched on the case, four cases away, wasn't a person at all.

The creature had short, smooth, black hair and resembled something between a cat and a chimpanzee except bigger. Its pointed ears twitched a little as it surveyed the room with big yellow eyes. It appeared to be wearing bib overalls.

In an instant, its head snapped in my direction, its inch-long claws squealed across the display case as it launched in my direction. It was fast! Too fast! It made the distance to me in two jumps, skipping the second case and jumping off the third. Clawed hands reached out for my throat as the creature's lips parted, showing a row of long, sharp, white teeth.

Not having time to pull the dagger out, all I could do was reach out and grab for the creature, and I got an ear and part of its fur-covered head. I sunk my fingers in as hard as I could, as a clawed hand ripped through the sleeve of my leather jacket. I pivoted, extending my arm to increase the momentum of the airborne, clawed projectile.

Throwing my weight into it, the creature's head hit the wall with a loud crack and a crunch. As I released, it slid down to the floor to be intercepted in the face by my boot. Another crunch. It was a solid hit, and with its head pinned between my boot and the wall, it slumped over not moving. *Oh no! move now!* Something was coming, I could hear it cutting through the air.

I pivoted the other way as the tomahawk drove into the wall where my head had been. Right behind it was the second creature, moving at the same speed as the tomahawk, and it was in front of me before I could think!

Throwing my forearm up to intercept the incoming teeth and claws, it hit my arm hard. As its teeth and claws wrapped around my blocking forearm, my hand was already pulling out the Kris for its sheath, but the damage was done, and the creature was already bearing down. The massive power of the bite sent pain all the way to my chest. AAAAH!

The pain was weakening my knees as I drove the Kris in hard through the bib overalls of my second attacker; its eyes slammed open wide as the blade protruded through the other side. The pain receded as I yanked the blade back out. The creature started to fall back, turning fast,I ran the blade hard along the side of the creature's neck, and it went deep.

I went to shield my eyes from the blood spray, but my action was cut short by five flying silver objects that came from the main hallway. *Shuriken!* I threw myself out of the way of the deadly flying stars. They missed by only a fraction of an inch, smashing the glass wall displays behind me. My hip caught the corner of the floor display case, throwing me over the top and leaving a throbbing pain in my hip. *Ouch! Ow! That hurt, no blood so far, at least not mine.*

I hit the floor with a thud. The other three intruders were in the room with me, and it didn't appear they were making a frontal assault as the others had. *Maybe they learned their lesson! Nope! The dirty little creeps are just trying to be sneaky now!* I jumped up off the floor and took a look over the case just in time to almost take a spear in the face that had been thrown from across the room.

OH, that was evil you little shits, now I'm gonna hurt ya! Another ax smashed into the side of the case I was hiding behind, shattering the front with a crash. *I had better come up with something pretty quick, this case won't take much more damage! Just breathe and think!* Exhaling a long breath, I closed my eyes for a second, and behind my eyelids I could see lines of what seemed to be energy running up the walls and to the fluorescent lights and to the cases.

That's electricity, I can see it, I feel it!

And the feeling got stronger, I could feel it running through the wires, I could feel it making the light. *I'm gonna pull it to those little asses and see how they like it.* I was hot! The pain had increased my temper, and now I was fuming mad. Reaching out, I felt as if I got a hold of the energy, capturing every bit of the invisible flowing material as I possibly could.

Another projectile smashed into the case, collapsing it. As I stood up and pulled with all of my will, there was a sharp crackle followed by a deafening boom as every case and every light in the room exploded, and tendrils of electricity came out of every source, bouncing and merging together in huge arcs, arcing off every metallic object in the room.

The temperature of the room increased instantly. I pulled harder. The electrical arcs sped across the celling, merging together into a huge lightning bolt that snapped to the floor with a boom, arcing through the creatures and across the floor, setting the carpet instantly on fire.

The creatures howled as the bolt blew them across the room, and only one got back up and went running for the main hallway. It fumbled with a pouch in his hands and threw some type of silver powder in the air. It shimmered like a mirror as the creature threw its burning body through it. The shimmering mirror disappeared, taking the creature with it.

The fire was the only light left as my hair started to lay back down as the static from the room dissipated. Smoke rose from the shoulders of my leather jacket, it was hot, the sweat ran down my face, and with a shaking hand, I wiped some from my burning eyes. *There! Take that!*

I walked over and leaned up against the smoking wall and charred paint.

I didn't care, I was still shaking from exertion. *What the..* my senses alerted me again, there were eight, no, ten.

No! I ran out the door, the intruders were popping up all over like blips on a radar. *None on the lower floors, but these ones are headed my way fast! Oh hell, I could be in trouble.*

I hurtled down the stairs, and the room at the bottom was dimly lit. The emergency lighting was still working here. As my eyes adjusted, I saw that the room was huge and full of all manner of war machinery; it was ancient but all of it seemed to be in perfect working condition.

I don't have much time, I gotta do something! I can't handle another fight like the last one!

Grabbing the first thing I could find, I rolled the massive cannon around and pointed it at the short hallway at the end of the stairs. It made a good bottleneck. Looking at the end of the 22-inch cannon opening, I could see the massive cannonball sitting in it, ready to go!

Oh my god, it's loaded! If they're gonna kill me, I'm taking as many of those bastards with me as I can! My temper kicked back up at the thought of it giving me renewed strength. Another cannon was in place, a ballista with a 10-foot arrow. *Gotta hurry, they're gonna be here soon.*

I could sense the group of twenty on its way, they were checking each room as they came, and they moved like a pack of wild dogs. *They're sticking together! Maybe, I made an impression, they learn quickly!* I moved another contraption over, and the square device has twenty-five slots in it, each housing a large nasty-looking arrow with just a jute string as the triggering device. It was cocked and ready to go by the look of it. I rolled it in place, targeting the entrance. *THAT ought to slow them down a bit! OH MY! Some speed fuse!*

I'm not entirely sure how I knew it was a speed fuse, whether it was my newly found intuition or a memory from my invisible past. The contraption that it was connected to was far too big to move into place. I collected the fuse and was about to run back to my line of defense. Then an idea struck. *If I tie the pull string fired weapons, the one cannon the recoil will set off the other devices!*

The plan sounded like a good one. I connected the cords to the cannon and attached the speed fuse. It was set. I looked around for something to light the fuse. *Nothing!* I could feel the panic rising in my stomach. *Only thirty seconds left and that mob will be coming down the stairs!* I could hear them now even without my enhanced hearing.

I checked the pockets of my leather jacket with a prayer, but the lower two pockets were empty. I unzipped the top right pocket and stuffed my hand in, there was something there.

I pulled it out, the green flame-shaped stone hung off the cord in my hand. It was warm, and inside sparked a tiny red flame no bigger than a grain of salt. I could feel it though, it was definitely fire.

Breaking my disbelief, I brought the stone close to the end of the fuse, and I reached into it with all of my being. It reacted! A small spurt of fire shot out and hit the fuse, I looked up and saw nothing but yellow eyes in the hallway. The fuse burned with a snap, lighting everything it was tied to all at once. I went deaf while flying back. The impact of the cannons going off in the enclosed area was tremendous. I never felt the ground before my world went dark.

I started to come around again. There were multiple voices, they were talking, and it seemed all at the same time. Someone had my shoulder and was lifting me up. "Just relax, I got you!" I cracked my eyes open a bit, and there was light, daylight! As my eyes adjusted, I was able to see a gaping hole. I was still in the basement, but it appeared that the explosion had taken out the wall and the dirt that had been banked partway up the concrete basement walls. People were moving stones out of the way and inspecting the damage. They didn't seem to pay us any mind.

My ears were still ringing, Sylus was looking down at me. "Welcome back, I'm glad to see you're okay!" I started to get up, and Sylus assisted a bit. "Where are those things" I looked around, feeling for a moment that I was in a dream, still a bit under the weather. "Oh, there is not much left of them, it seems you dispatched them with EXTREME prejudice! The damage IS quite extensive! A bit overkill perhaps! But that doesn't matter, you managed okay. I do have to admit, this was a bit more complicated than I had expected."

"Sylus!" I caught sight of a young lanky fellow with glasses, wearing a tan tweed suit coat and a pair of jeans, working his way through the rubble, and coming down the stairs. "Sylus, you got to have a look at this!" He got to the bottom of the stairs and caught sight of me. The open-mouthed, dumbfounded expression on his face stayed there far too long for it to be dramatic.

"This is the girl who destroyed the place?" "Now Thomas! You need to be a little more polite! You wouldn't have done any better!" Sylus was scowling at him. It was the first time I had ever seen anything from Sylus that resembled annoyance. "I believe she did a very good job, under the circumstances. And without requesting compensation, which is less than can be said for you."

Thomas glanced down with a short "Harrumph" and turned to Sylus. "Anyway, the Kratz were all carrying these." He was handing him a small drawstring, black leather pouch. As Sylus opened the pouch, I could see tiny flecks of silver power rise from the opening. "That stuff is so rare Sylus, it's only found in one place!" Sylus was examining the pouch, "That means he's found it, then."

"How can that be Sylus? We can't even find that mine!" "I don't know, but he's starting to gain power again. You know fair well that Kratz are his favorite toys." Thomas let out a shudder. "I hate those things!" "How is it that they were not able to read her?" Thomas made a gesture in my direction. "They tried, but it was too little too late. Like I said before, Susan is more than capable."

Another grunt from Thomas. "Well thank you, Thomas, for your assistance, you will be okay taking charge of the cleanup efforts, won't you?" Thomas turned around and headed back up the stairs, looking annoyed. "Kratz, huh." I looked at Sylus, and he was peering in the pouch again. "What exactly is that stuff?" I questioned. "It's way powder. An easy way to travel anywhere you can perceive, as it's not restricted by size or distance. Dangerous stuff, but very useful."

He took a pen out of his pocket, put the end in the pouch, then flicked it in the air. The silver powder spread, making a mirror-looking area that hovered in front of him. "Let's go, shall we?" Sylus made a motion to the shimmering mirrored area. I walked through. My foot landed on the carpet as I stepped into Sylus' office. It was instant, no distance, just stepping from one place to another. Moving to the side, Sylus stepped through and the silvery portal closed. *That stuff is amazing!*

I slumped into a chair. "And these Kratz things, what are they? And this guy you're talking about, who is he?" Sylus chuckled, "Well one thing at a time, first of all, Kratz are a creation of an individual called Temeculeck. He is the individual that we were talking about. That fellow has a very powerful set of abilities but tends to use them negatively. He doesn't care to fit into society and be a positive influence to the universe, and he's mostly interested in how many rules of nature and reality he can effectively break. Not the nicest fellow."

Sylus took a seat behind his desk. "What he has done is effectively given us trouble for years!" Sylus shook his head. "He's very clever and very hard to catch and isn't too concerned about the lives of others. He's somewhere in between Voldemort and Dr. Frankenstein. He likes his power and pets." My body was aching, and my head was pounding as I sat exhausted in the office trying to recap the events that had taken place. I was quickly realizing that there was a lot to this new reality that I was gonna have to learn and get used to.

It sounds like this guy is real trouble, but strangely, I know who Voldemort is and Dr. Frankenstein, I know exactly which movies they are in, but no recollection of when I watched them. What happened! In all of this, I haven't gotten one lousy clue as to who I really am. It's like I was born into this world complete with a full library of information at my disposal. Whatever happened to me was not good, I'm sure of that, even with these newfound abilities, I know just as much about myself as when I woke up out in that godforsaken desert.

"You should probably get some rest and clean up a bit. You look like you have had enough for one day." I was busy examining the area on my forearm where the Krat had bit me, I was sure I was going to find gaping holes where the teeth went clean to the bone, but nothing. Not even a bruise! Both the jacket and leather shirt had no sign of damage, it was like nothing ever happened. *Where's that necklace I had it in my hand when...*then I noticed the warmth on my chest- I was wearing it.

CHAPTER NINE

Retaliation

"I see you found the little gift I left in your jacket, I hope it came in handy," Sylus said, shooting me a knowing look, as I subconsciously reached up to touch the small, flame-shaped stone hanging around my neck. "Yes, it was very useful." "Where did you get such a thing?" I asked, taking my hand away from the warmth resonating from the stone.

"I made it. I have found it useful in the past, and I thought I would pass it on to you." I looked at Sylus as he looked down at his desk as if to examine something important, color creeping into his cheeks.

"Soooo, this way powder stuff, you say is pretty rare?" "Yes, that kind of material comes from a different plane of reality, some places around the world have a thinner lining where it allows seepage from other realities to contaminate it. They're called by many names, sacred areas, power hubs, nodes, dimensional gates, ley lines, and the list goes on. Each is different but has shared effects, all are parts of quantum physics and have a connection to the time-space continuum. Science is always arguing that something has to be one way or the other, but the reality is that both things exist and they directly affect one another in infinite ways."

"In most cases, both theories are correct. They just like to argue, nothing is JUST one way or the other. If that were the case, we would have quit finding new discoveries hundreds of years ago." Sylus paused a moment. "And that's the short answer."

"So, this Temeculeck dude has found one of those areas and that's where he's getting this stuff?" Sylus nodded, "That's what we are thinking, but we just can't figure out where." Sylus looked disturbed. "How do we find this guy?" "We don't. Like I said, he's very hard to catch. And if we did catch him, he's going to be an issue to handle. You probably should get some rest, you have had quite a day! Don't be too concerned, we will figure things out when the time comes."

It was getting late, the large grandfather clock near the dining room was starting to chime as I left Sylus's office. *8:00 P.M., today has been a blur!* As I walked to my room, the fatigue hit me, thoughts of food entered my mind and were then squashed immediately by the thought of a shower and sleep. *I have memories now, who would have thought they would be so bizarre! I can't imagine any other memories that I may have that would be as interesting or exciting!*

I was absorbed. All I could think about was the events that had transpired, and they ran over and over in my mind like a movie that I watched, again and again, never getting sick of it. As the hot water from the shower poured over my aching body, I took the time to look for damage.

Not a scratch, all of that, and not even as much as a bruise! It has to be those comfy leathers, I know it! And they were comfy! Laughing to myself, I thought about wearing them to bed. I got dressed and curled up in bed, looking at the tiny spark floating in the stone of the necklace that hung around my neck.

My dreams became fuzzy like an old tv that had lost signal; my mind was full of nothing but static as I snapped awake. A loud crack sounded from outside the door, I heard Missy shout something from outside. Another loud crack. My senses didn't seem to be working right, I grabbed my Kris from its sheath and ran to the door. The hallway was a scene of utter chaos, as dark shadowy creatures swooped and dove like bats after a moth. The creatures did resemble bats; they looked like black smoke, surrounded by a red aura, dark smoky tendrils seemed to trail behind them.

Sylus and Missy were all batting frantically, and there was another loud crack, Missy Staggered back four steps, and she had a white-knuckled grip on the blunderbuss as a blue crystal-like material flew from the barrel, lodging into the walls and ceiling, and taking out five of the flying creatures with it. She was in the middle of the hall to my right while Sylus was at the end to the left. He was moving so fast that my eyes could hardly keep up.

The sword in his hands flashed back and forth at amazing speed, along with a crackle and a sizzling sound as the creatures disintegrated off the end of his blade. He caught sight of me "He tracked us, I took care of it, but too late!" he said breathlessly, as the sword sliced through two more of the shadowy forms. I knew who HE was- apparently, we had gained a lot of attention.

"Don't let them touch you, they will burn right through you!"

I could tell by the damage in the hall that he was not exaggerating, there were holes in the wall and on the floor where the creatures burned all the way through the granite tile. I reached out with my mind and got nothing but static, the low crackling buzz that was coming from these creatures was jamming my brain somehow and had saturated the house. "Sylus! Nothing is working!"

"Most skills won't work! You got to kill them by hand!" Sylus jumped, putting both feet on the wall, doing a partial cartwheel, severing two of the creatures that had targeted his legs, while another was flying for his head from behind him. He flipped the katana blade to the rear and bowed, holding the sharp edge of the blade straight up over his shoulder. The creature intercepted the blade with a crackle and was gone.

Another had cut right through the wall and headed for missy. It was behind her, and she was franticly trying to reload the Blunderbuss. I threw the Kris, and it sped across the hall, creature just inches from its target. The creature was gone before my dagger buried itself into the wall next to her. I reached out through space to retrieve the dagger and found nothing but the buzzing static that was blocking me. I made a run for it, darting across the hall.

"Susan, lookout," Bolt's voice rang out from the other end of the hall, and he was running toward Missy. In mid-stride, he threw a small glass ball the size of a large marble. I ducked as the small glass ball flew over my head, striking the creature that has just rounded the corner next to me. The ball exploded with a pop on impact. There was a bright flash of light that seemed to tear the shadowy creature into pieces. I pulled my dagger from the wall as Bolt passed us. "Run! They're coming!"

I caught a glance of Missy pulling a hand full of sand out of the shot pouch and dumped it down the barrel of the hand cannon as I turned to retreat. "Come on, Missy!" Missy braced herself. I could hear the oncoming wave of creatures, their staticky sounds filling the hallway. The swarm was huge and disintegrated four feet of the wall as it rounded the corner, tearing through studs and sheet rock, turning them to ash. The hall was nothing but a mass of black wings, the red aura lighting up the walls just before they were disintegrated.

Boom! The bark of the blunderbuss echoed in the hall, and a gigantic spray of water came out of the barrel, freezing everything it came in contact with. Missy was thrown into me by the recoil. She immediately turned and ran after catching her balance. Sounds of breaking ice came from the hall behind me as the creatures dropped to the ground and shattered. But there were still more coming.

That thinned them out! At least they're not tearing up the house anymore! Sylus *was* in the lead, and he had cut through three more of the bat-like creatures with one deft movement that was so fast the blade looked as if it were made of light. It left tracers in the air in the shape of a triangle that seemed to linger for a moment. Missy was wadding up a hand full of grass that she had taken out of that strange shot pouch and stuffing it down the barrel of the gun as she ran.

Sylus jumped and spun, swinging his blade in a wide arch. As he turned, the blade connected with what would have been the head of another incoming shadow and landed facing us. "Get behind me"! he yelled. Bolt had passed him and appeared to be watching the hall at Sylus's back. Missy passed and squatted into a seated position, resting that cannon across her knee and lining up on the hall, Sylus reached down and touched her shoulder. "Just wait for it Missy! I'll tell you when."

I got behind Sylus while he was pointing at something. I turned around and realized what he was pointing to. Adrenaline pumping and my sight going into tunnel vision, I had run right by that pretty little plant that set on the table in the hall. *Audrey? Why is he so interested in that cute little plant, it is adorable and all but really?*

Sylus just stood there, still, watching the shadowy shapes glide down the hallway toward us. The little plant's vines were curled back like a mantis's legs, and it was indeed looking down the hall in the direction of the creatures. The tiny vines seemed to leap out at startling speed, snatching seven of the flying shadows out of the air and pulling them to itself. The pods snapped open and attached to the creatures, ripping the red aura from them, dissolving them to nothing in an instant.

"Fire!" Sylus gave Missy her cue and the blunderbuss cracked again, sending a barrage of green needles flying down the hall, piercing through the remaining creatures, sounding like a thousand darts hitting a dartboard. Immediately, the static was gone. Missy scrambled back to her feet, shaking off the recoil.

I felt a sense of vertigo as all of my heightened senses kicked back in. The difference was now very noticeable to me, it was as if I were in a soundproof room with no lights when someone opened the door to a party happening on the other side. *Wow! Now I know how "Normal" feels!* I had no recollection of normal, but what I was feeling prior was definitely lacking, and the disconnection from true reality was terrible. *Is this what regular people feel? How can people live in such a state? You can't miss what you have never had, I guess.* Turning my thoughts to introspection, I had a lot that I didn't miss, and for a short minute, I was glad.

"That could have gone much worse," Sylus said with a sigh of relief. He walked over to the little plant on the table and touched one of the vines that were reaching out to him. "Thank you, Audrey, you were a great help" He smiled at the plant and the plant seemed to respond back with a strange flourish of vines, and its pods seemed to bow in acknowledgment.

Sylus rose an open hand over his head and closed it. The green needles sticking in the walls and ceiling turned to powder and drifted to the gaping holes and gashes in the walls and floor, effectively repairing the damage with the exact material type and color. Dumbfounded, I shut my gaping mouth and tried to regain my composure.

How the hell was that possible! But I knew! I had seen the material break down to a molecular level and reform its structure, I could feel the extension of Sylus's mind as he chose the way the material would reform. He had touched it the same way I had reached out and grabbed the baseball at a distance. *I see it! I believe it! But I don't get it. That was complex, he used many types of senses and awareness's in conjunction to produce the effect.*

I could feel his awareness of things down to the electrons, protons, and neutrons. It wasn't good enough to just know how things went together, he had a relationship with it, he was part of it. The depth of how he was feeling was so personal that it made my eyes water up from the emotion that he felt. He was part of reality, and at that point, I understood there was a big difference between knowing and being.

Sylus lowered his hand and motioned us to follow as he walked back down the hall. The door to his office was partially off the hinges, so he opened what was left, shaking his head in disgust. "this is going to take a lot of fixing," he muttered. Setting his sword down on his desk, Sylus dropped into his chair, rubbing his forehead with his thumb and forefinger.

"What happened Sylus? Where did all those things come from" "Temeculeck attached his mind to the way powder containers, and it was well shielded. I only realized it when he has connected with them. This house is neither here nor there, but when there is a tracker involved, it is like a beacon that gave him a location. He sent those creatures through before I could sever it. He probably thinks we are dead, at least we can hope."

Everyone else was seated except me, my adrenaline was still pumping from the experience. I realized that I was just standing there fidgeting. Taking a seat, I tried to let go of my anxiety. "Nothing else to do but clean this mess up I guess, he didn't kill us but he certainly messed things up for a bit!" "Why don't you all get some food, and I'll clean up." We all nodded and headed for the dining hall. Missy was still clutching the blunderbuss like it was a baby. "Is that the gun from the display room, Missy?" I questioned. Bolt was the one to speak up.

"That's kinda my fault, I was just showing her some of the more interesting items that have been collected here ,and I thought I would take it out to show her how it worked, for training purposes you know, and then, while I was teaching her how to use it in the practice room, things went crazy, and we had to take drastic measures. I was just helping her with training, she was never in danger. Well, at least not until the attack."

"Okay bolt, you're not on trial. I was just curious if that was the same gun I saw." "Oh yes! It's the same one, a matter transmuting blunderbuss and a materialization shot pouch. It's been imbued with the ability to materialize, all types of material, you never know what you're gonna get and then when you put it in the gun it. . ." "Sure! that's very interesting and all but where's the kitchen?" I couldn't really blame Bolt for being so wound up but, *Good lord!*

When we got to the dining room, Bolt directed us through two large swinging doors that opened both ways. They were wood and the intricate carving on them matched the rest of the house. The kitchen was fantastic, equipped with restaurant-worthy equipment all stainless steel with granite counters and an island, plus a huge stainless-steel refrigerator and walk-in freezer. It made me want to cook something just because.

The fridge was full, so I produced the makings of a ham and turkey sandwich, along with some recently baked bread from the huge pantry. Missy was not parting with that gun any time soon; she held it as she grabbed some cheese and crackers with her empty hand. "I'll put that stuff away for you, Susan." Bolt said as I put my sandwich on a plate. He was following suit with the ham and turkey idea.

I sat down at the table in the dining room and started to eat, for the first time I noticed I was still in my nightclothes as the grandfather clock chimed four times. *Four in the monring?! You have got to be kidding me, I'm never getting back to sleep and I'm not staying in my nightclothes either.*

I finished my food and put my plate back in the kitchen. *I wonder who cleans this place?* I thought as I walked out the door back to the dining room and proceeded back to my room. I turned into the hallway expecting to see the massive damage that was done by our unwelcome guests, but that was not the case.

The hall was completely repaired not even as much as a speck of dust remained of the unbelievable chaos that had occurred just an hour ago. As I entered my room, I had one mission on my mind. *I'm getting back into those comfy leathers.*

C H A P T E R T E N

Reality 101

have to figure out how he does that. Thinking about how Sylus had repaired the walls with just a gesture. *If I can do that, I will be really impressed with myself.* I wanted it bad!

I slipped on my preferred clothing and heard Missy and Bolt head back to their rooms. Taking a look into the hall and seeing no one, I headed off down the hall, stopping for a minute at the room with the displays. *Still gone, she's going to sleep with that gun.* I would, after the events that transpired!

Going down the hall the familiar change in wall material from plaster to rivetted steel made me smile. *I think it was the second door to the right.* I walked up to the keypad, pressing the button, and the door slid open. The sense of a thousand materials hit me like a brick again, making my headache. The door slid shut, my head was a buzz, there was just too much to take in, everything was jumbled together. It was like being at a concert with a party going on, talking to six people and trying to remember what you ate on a Tuesday last month.

This is going to be a lot harder than I thought. I cleaned off a spot on the floor in the middle of the room and sat. *Somehow, I have to get past all this clutter!* I got as comfortable as the floor would allow and closed my eyes. Everything that I was sensing was screaming at one another, I took in a deep breath and let it out slowly, then I took another.

The warm air from the exhale touching my lips made the air seem more real and more tangible. It was solid, it had mass, feeling the pressure difference

6 5

in my chest as I inhaled, I followed the invisible material in and out of my lungs, I could feel my blood pulse and my heartbeat with every exhale. The yelling in my head had stopped, everything just was, nothing was jockeying for position in my thoughts.

Just one thing, only one item at a time! I kept saying it to myself as I began to slowly reach out. *Sand, just sand, looking for sand only.* And I found plenty, I could feel it mixed under and in the other materials, but it stood out like a red hat when everyone else is wearing white. I could feel each grain as if I had it between my fingers, see it as if through a microscope. *Now reach out and grab some.*

Feeling the same as reaching out for the baseball, I pulled as much of the sand as my mind could hold onto. Drawing it out of the other materials, I pulled it into a pile in front of me. Cracking my eyes open a little bit, I examined the coffee can worth of sand that I had managed to collect in the neat pile in front of me. It was all sand and nothing else. *Good! Well, now let's see if I can do something with it!*

Closing my eyes again, I focused on the pile, feeling it again, letting it speak to me, each grain was dirty glass. I could sense and feel the presence of the other minerals and materials in it, contaminating it. *Do the same thing with that, just reach in and draw out the impurities.* Taking another peek to see how well I had done, I cracked my eyes open to find the sand, perfectly clear. The beautiful quartz crystals gleamed in the light. My heart jumped with emotion at the spectacle. I felt like I had done something truly extraordinary, but I wasn't finished yet! Taking another deep breath, I closed my eyes again.

It's all the same just put it together, it wants to be together. I allowed the feeling of the beautiful sand to come together. The door opened with a hiss. I jumped so hard I almost tipped backward from my seated position. The sense of all the materials in a jumbled mess crashed back into my mind.

Ahh, my head! The headache was back in full measure as I turned to Sylus, now standing inside of the door. He looked tired, I could see where the perspiration had crept through his dark blue button-up shirt, making it darker in some areas. His hair seemed a bit curlier, probably from the humidity. His sleeves were rolled up, and the moisture of the shirt gave off hints of the muscle underneath. *Oh lord! Quit looking!* My face was on fire, again! "I thought I would find you here," he said as he turned his head and looked around the room. I was quite sure that he was trying to ignore my face, which made it all the worse.

"I see you're having some success with it," he said, pointing at the pile of sand. I was happy to turn my attention back to what I was doing before he scared the hell out of me. On the pile of sand sat a chunk of glass about the size of an egg; the edges were rough and unformed, but nonetheless pretty, catching the light with a shimmer. Again, I was excited and couldn't stop the grin that was growing on my face.

"I am, but I just don't understand how! Not that I'm complaining." "I suppose the best way I can explain is how much force does it really take to move an atom? Hardly anything, we move them all the time. You really don't know what control you have if you can't, or choose not to, make a connection with it. Everything emits energy of all types all the time- heat, magnetics, brain waves to name a few, but in most cases, we have no connection to it so we have no control, even if it is produced by us for us."

"Some have more control than others, but it's limited to what they think they know or accept. It's been proven over time, our reality changes all the time with the progress of knowledge." He bent down and picked up a stone off the floor.

"Just look at the world now compared to 200 years ago, people do more extraordinary things on accident than on purpose. That is because we battle all the time with what we are taught, we fight doubt, we don't accept things, and most people live in a state of disbelief that they have created for themselves. If we can't see it, touch it, or use it, it just doesn't exist. And that is far from the reality of things. I would think people would have figured that out over the years, but they are content living in their self-created boxes." He looked at me, reading me to see if I actually understood.

"It makes perfect sense to me, if you don't have a grip on true reality, how can you be a functioning part of it? You have no control over what you don't have a connection to." And that truly was the simple answer. Now, after saying it, it was just as simple as that. He nodded. "Just keep that in mind, we choose more than we really know," he said as he turned to the door. I did notice the stone was no longer in his hand as he started to leave the room. "Good night, or should I say, good morning," he said, shooting a grin over his shoulder at me. The door slid shut behind him.

It really does make sense when it comes right down to it, I suppose I'm quite for-tunate to have been put in this position in life, I really wonder if I were to figure out my past will it affect where I'm at now? Will I lose my newfound abilities? I really don't want to part with any of them. Then, there they were, worry and doubt coming into rain on my parade.

Well, that is one thing I'm not going to believe! I just hoped that I had con-vinced myself of it. I turned back to my little sand pile and bent to pick up my creation. *What the!* Beside my piece of glass sat a dark blue flower. I thought for a moment it was a pansy with pretty black on blue designs, but at a closer look, I saw that it had ten petals and the center was an intricate orange spiral, the black on the petals did not have a pattern, it just went here and there ran-domly. It was a beautiful work of art.

Immediately, I felt my cheeks catch fire. Another thing to add to my grow-ing list of things that I had never seen before. I picked up my prizes and walked to the door. Returning to my room, I set the piece of glass and the flower on my nightstand with a smile of satisfaction and sprawled out on my bed.

I was tired. I think it was more mental fatigue than physical, but the adrenaline that I was on a constant diet of recently was taking its toll on me as I lay there staring at the ceiling. *Is it going to slow down around here?* I was hoping not, but my mind was at maximum intake, and for days, I had been on a high-octane life rush. It felt like I was trying to catch up on life due to not having a memory of anything prior.

If I never find out who I really am, I can be content with that. This life is beyond imaginable. However, that didn't mean that I wasn't going to try, as my curiosity would never allow me to forget that at one point there was a life that I had lived prior to this, and looking for clues to what that life was seemed to be in my very nature.

I had no sense of time here, being neither here nor there. The house was definitely separated from things, due to Sylus's fancy safety precautions. So, all I could sense was the internal and a lot of that seemed to be blocked off. And that was a good thing, too, as I thought of the room full of material that had a knack of giving me a headache.

I had begun to pay attention to the clock by the dining room. It was the only reference to the time that I had, the low chime telling me that it was seven in the morning just made me feel all the more tired. *I wonder if there is a library here, I suppose I'll have to look for it.* And that was the last idea that I had before I drifted off into the dark swirl of my subconscious.

Dong, Dong, Dong. Dong! *Four o'clock,* I thought as I rolled over onto my belly, scooting forward to let my arms hang off the bed. *It better not be a.m.* I knew that it wasn't, I could hear people talking in the dining room. Feeling a little groggy from getting that much sleep during the day hours, I trudged off to the door and into the hall. *I smell tacos! Oh god, I hope it's tacos! Ooooh, it better be tacos!* I arrived at the dining room, and I was not disappointed. *Yep! It's tacos!*

Everyone was dishing up the food when I entered. "You all are lucky I woke up! If I would have missed out on tacos, it would not have been pretty!" There was a pause, then everyone exploded into laughter. "We would not have let you go without," Sylus chuckled. Everyone needed a good laugh, as none of us had much time for humor, and it was a pleasant change. I sat down at the table, listening to Missy and Bolt go on about the battle and other extraordinary items that may or may not exist in Sylus's house.

Sylus just shook his head, smiled, and continued eating. "So, Susan would you be interested in helping me with an issue that recently happened, involving a missing person? We will be able to start our investigation in about two weeks after the authorities have finished nosing around." Sylus said after he had finished eating. "Sure! Sounds interesting! Not like anything could occur in the meantime." Missy and Bolt started giggling profusely. "Touché, Susan, Touché."